UPTOWN OGRE

MONSTERVILLE, USA, BOOK 6

AVA ROSS

*For my parents who
always believed I could do this.*

SERIES BY AVA

Mail-Order Brides of Crakair

Brides of Driegon

Fated Mates of the Ferlaern Warriors

Fated Mates of the Xilan Warriors

Holiday with a Cu'zod Warrior

Galaxy Games

Alien Warrior Abandoned

Beastly Alien Boss

Bride of the Fae

A Sci-Fi Holiday Tail

Monsterville, USA

Monster on Board
(co-written with Alana Khan)

A Monster Worth Fighting For
(Monster Between the Sheets)

Love at First Orc

Third Galaxy on the Left

Monster Mate Hunt

You can find her books on Amazon.

UPTOWN OGRE

A suit-wearing ogre is pretending to be my boyfriend, and I think I'm falling in love.

After being ousted from my small town by an underhanded wedding planner who is also now my ex, I moved to Monsterville for a fresh start. There, I find myself in direct competition with the hottest ogre in town, Raze. He's too cocky and snobby for his own good, and he wears designer suits and ties all the time. I sometimes wonder if he wears them to bed.

When my ex shows up in Monsterville, determined to win me back, Raze steps in, offering to pretend he's my boyfriend and business partner. Only when my ex tries to outbid me on a royal fae wedding do I agree. With our combined forces, Raze and I will win the job and send my ex packing.

The more time I spend with Raze, however, the more I wish he was my real boyfriend. Can I convince him that an ogre and a human are the perfect monster match?

Uptown Ogre is set in the Monsterville, USA Series. Each book is standalone and is best if read in order (see below). Expect romantic hijinks with monsters, heat, and a happily ever after.

Check out the entire Monsterville world!

Candy for my Orc Boss
Orc Me Baby One More Time
Gargoyles Just Want to Have Fun
Don't Go Knotting My Heart
Whose Bed Have Your Claws Been Under?
Uptown Ogre
Oops, I Elf'd it Again
My Orc-y Breaky Heart
Hold Me Closer, Fiery Phoenix
Who Let the Demon Out?

ELISA

Raze, my ogre wedding planner competition who happened to own an office across from mine, opened the door to *my* office and stepped inside. He brought a welcome gust of spring mountain air and his unwelcome, surly attitude.

I hadn't seen him since Christmas, when we formed a truce only long enough to plan the wedding for his cousin and my friend. After that, we returned to Monsterville and tried to ignore each other.

He hated me. If only I could hate him. Leave it to me to form a crush on the guy who ran the only other wedding planner business in town. The last time something like that happened . . . Well, that was why I'd moved to Monsterville for a fresh start.

Despite his perpetual scowl, I struggled not to notice how well this ogre body filled out his suit. At five-nine, I was tall, but he towered over me by at least a foot. A girl should be turned off by his copper skin and knobby ogre head, let alone his horns, but I couldn't look away. He kept his hair cut short, which fit with his business ogre image.

Most of the monsters living in town were equally broad and muscular. I should hook up with one of them, right?

Now that monsters had melted out of the woods and clawed their way up from beneath the ground, joining human society, I could have my pick from hot, winged gargoyles, feisty centaurs with more than one . . . ahem, and even a few grumpy trolls eager to make me pay an interesting price to cross their bridge.

Why couldn't I fixate on one of them instead of Raze?

"May I help you?" I asked him, my voice higher pitched than I liked.

"Finish what you're doing." He waved a manicured hand to my clients sitting across the desk from me, and his long tail swept back and forth behind him. "I'll wait. We can speak after you're finished."

The woman gawked at him, and I could see why. Even if he was a snob, he kind of blew you away.

"Check out the ogre," the bride, Margie, whispered to her orc fiancé, Vrok. "You should wear a suit like that to the wedding."

Her family was well-connected in town, and scoring this job would give my fledgling business the boost it needed. Instead of sitting at my desk forlornly staring at my silent phone, I would be booking one wedding after another. If I was awarded this job and the fae wedding I was about to bid on, my reputation would be set.

Vrok patted the cute dragonette sitting on his shoulder, and it preened before shooting Margie a scowl—or what I took for a scowl. She ignored it, which was odd since his family raised them, and he and Margie were engaged. You'd think she'd be interested in the creature since they were so closely linked to his family.

When I first saw his dragonette, I was mesmerized by the tiny creature's golden scales and the spit of flames it shot my way in affection.

Vrok turned to peer over his shoulder at Raze, keeping his voice low when he spoke with his fiancée. "Do you think I'd look good in a black suit with a starched shirt and tie?" He didn't sound convinced, though he should get used to the idea because other than the color, Margie had made it clear he'd be wearing a suit at their wedding.

"Trust me." She tapped her long nails on his arm. "I understand things like this when you . . . sometimes don't."

Uh-oh. Was there trouble between them? I'd hate to lose this job, but their happiness came first.

He nodded. "I'll try." And that was all anyone could ask for in a relationship.

As for the stiff ogre still standing in my doorway, I'd yet to see Raze dressed in anything but designer suits. Did he ever let down his hair, so to speak, and wear something casual?

Doubtful. I could picture him sitting upright on his porch or deck or whatever he might have at his home, still dressed like a billionaire businessman. No beer in his hand. No games set up on the lawn. And definitely no cute little doggies or dragonettes curling up on his lap.

For all I knew, he slept in a suit. I could barely resist the urge to stride over to him and loosen his tie, maybe undo a couple of the top buttons of his shirt and expose his chest.

Oh, and tug off his glasses so I could stare into his gorgeous green eyes.

Sadly, my inconsistent crush was not returned. Inconsistent, that is, because I went from wanting to kiss him to an insatiable urge to kill him.

I had nothing against ogres in general, just one very irritating ogre wedding planner who was determined to drive me out of business. Five months ago, when I moved to Monsterville and set up shop, he'd done his best to make me leave town, reminding me too much of why I'd closed my prior business and slunk here.

"So," I said to my clients, "you said you want to serve pink pasta with a pink-colored alfredo sauce." I struggled not to cringe. The customer was always right and Raze was listening. I had to show him I could provide a valuable service.

Handling this well would show the fae family I was the perfect planner for their upcoming royal wedding. They'd accept my bid, and my position as the reigning wedding planner in town would be secured.

Raze leaned against the wall beside the door and watched me, his arms crossing on his chest.

"As you can tell, my fiancée really loves pink," Vrok

said. I got the impression he was trying not to cringe. "If it makes Margie happy, I'm all about pink."

Margie leaned forward. "I was thinking of pink balloons and using some of that shimmery draping cloth as an archway when we enter the reception."

Raze released an odd sound, and I shot him a glare. Really, couldn't he come back when I wasn't busy? Or a year from now when I was completely established and could look down my nose at him instead of the other way around?

We'd been adversaries from the moment we met, when we were forced to co-organize the Christmas wedding. My friend Monica hired me to plan her side of the wedding to her ogre fiancé, Trevor. Trevor hired his snooty ogre cousin, Raze, to help me coordinate the weekend events. We'd spent half the time arguing and the rest of the time dreaming up what we could argue about next.

I couldn't imagine why my friend Paige suggested he liked me.

Raze cleared his throat as if he suspected I was daydreaming about his muscles. I had been earlier, but I wasn't now.

Margie grinned and patted Vrok's arm again. "Yes, I want lots of pink." She leaned against his side, linking their fingers. "Pink tablecloths and pink flowers."

"Ah," I said. "Perhaps with white baby's breath to break up the pink?"

Margie frowned. "Oh, no, we want everything to be pink."

I nodded, though I was trying to figure out how we could keep their reception from looking like a Pepto Bismol explosion. "The walls and floor of your venue won't be pink, of course."

Margie frowned and her voice lifted to a screech. "Why can't they be pink too?"

"Because we're only renting the room for the day," Vrok said, and I admired his patience. "Their next clients might prefer another color."

She blinked slowly at him as if she was seeing him for the first time.

"You could drape cloth on the floor and walls," she said, shooting a glance toward Raze, who continued to watch us. Didn't he have his own clients to chat with? "Other wedding planners have said they could do this," she added.

Damn him, was he poaching on my client? The ink was barely dry on my contract with Margie and Vrok. They were still within the one-week back-out window. To succeed in my new business, I needed every job I could get. I was barely making the rent on my office as it is.

I shot Raze a warning glare, receiving only a lifted unibrow look in exchange.

"Let me speak with your wedding venue," I said quickly. "I'm sure something can be arranged."

"Maybe . . ." Vrok shook his head.

"What?" Margie snapped his way.

"Nothing." He slumped in his chair.

I tugged my list over to make sure we went through

the rest of the items on my agenda. "Pink champagne, naturally."

Margie's smile returned, and my pulse lowered to a more normal level.

"In addition to pink pasta and alfredo sauce, I'll ensure they serve rosy bread with stained butter. I spoke with Storm, the wolf shifter catering the event, and he's excited about the radish-beet salad he'll prepare to go with the main course."

"Yay." Margie wiggled in her seat, clapping her hands.

"And the baker has confirmed your pink cake," I said.

"Our day is going to be so special." Margie said, overcome with excitement.

Growing up, I'd dreamed of finding someone to love who'd show me the same affection Vrok did for Margie, not the stilted coldness my parents displayed to each other—and most of the time, me.

In my teen years, I'd spent so much time drawing wedding gowns and picturing venues, plus making sketches and lists of what would make up the perfect wedding that it made sense for me to study hospitality management and business in college. After that, I got my certification and opened my business, only to have Love & Lace, my ex's chain wedding planner company, use our relationship to undercut my prices. He shouldered me out of business, and I had no choice but to set up shop somewhere new.

I hated to think Raze could be planning to do the same thing.

A town the size of Monsterville could support two wedding planners. He needed to learn how to share.

"Is there anything else?" Margie asked, standing. "I have a gown fitting appointment in ten minutes."

I'd made the arrangements. "No, that should be it for now. I'll reach out with any questions."

"Thank you."

"I'll let you know how the fitting goes," Margie said as she and Vrok started toward the front door.

"Take pictures," I called out after them.

"No pictures," Vrok said. "Not today, that is."

"I told you this was what I wanted," Margie ground out. They stopped near Raze, who watched them, his head snapping back and forth like this was a prime tennis match and he had a front-row seat.

"If you're not willing to let the photographer take pictures today, I'm calling it quits," Margie said.

"Really?" Vrok's thick brow drew together, and his spine stiffened. His dragonette fluttered its wings before settling. "You'd do something like that?"

"Vrok?" Margie bellowed.

"Yes?" He held his spine tight. I had to hand it to him; he had the stiff upper lip he'd need with Margie.

She wrenched off the ring from her left finger and threw it at him. It smacked his chest before falling, clinking on the tile floor. "We're over."

With that, she stormed from the room.

Vrok forlornly looked from me to Raze before stooping down to pick up the ring. "I'm sorry. I guess . . .

the wedding's off. I'll, um . . . You can keep the deposit." He eased around Raze and left.

Damn. I slumped back in my seat. One job gone, just like that.

Raze huffed. "He's better off without her, I think."

I saw red.

Standing, I rounded my desk and marched right up to Raze. "Why are you inside my office?" It was a struggle not to drool over his chiseled jawline and thick thighs. Why couldn't I shrug off my crush?

"Way to go with Margie and Vrok."

"Don't rub it in, though you're right that it's probably for the best." I wrenched my hair off my face and rese-cured it at my nape in the ponytail I'd made this morning it kept slipping out of. "Tell me what you want."

"Is that a way to greet a friend?" he asked in a sardonic, lofty tone. "We have something to discuss." Brushing past me, he took the chair Vrok had just vacated.

With a sigh deflating my lungs, I followed, sitting behind my desk once more.

My phone chimed, and I scowled at it before scrolling into the text message. Grr. It was from Harris, my ex.

I want you back, he texted. *I miss you. Can we talk?*

No, I quickly replied. *Leave me alone forever.* I turned off my phone and shoved it into a drawer.

"Welcome," I told Raze with pretend cheer. "What brings you here today, Raze?"

"I have a proposition for you," he said in a grumbly, growly voice that should make irritation flash through me. Instead, it made me long to drape myself across a bed—naked—while he climbed all over me.

"What might that be?" I asked, cocking my head.

"Someone's put in a low bid on the fae royal wedding."

"You *didn't*," I fumed, slamming my fist on my desk.

He huffed. "I'd like to get the job as much as you, but my bid will be honest."

I flopped back in my chair. "We're the only wedding planners in town. Who put in the other bid?"

"Love & Lace."

My damn ex's company. With branches all over the state, he could toss out low bids and spread the loss across the entire business.

I was sunk. There was no way I'd win this important job, and after losing Margie and Vrok's wedding, I was going to need to eat ramen for the rest of the month.

"He . . ." I blinked hard, trying not to cry. How could my ex do this? I loved Monsterville. I didn't want to move again.

I wanted to snap at Raze for watching me with a sardonic gleam in his eyes, but I held it inside. It wasn't his fault. There was no need to snarl at him. I'd save that for my ex.

"So, Elisa," Raze said. "What would you think of combining our businesses?"

CHAPTER 2

RAZE

"What did you say?" Elisa sputtered. "Why would we want to do something like that?"

Why indeed?

"I'm fairly confident the fae family will accept my bid," I said, watching her. This was something I did more often than I should. If I was wise, I'd sit back and let her fail. She'd leave Monsterville as quickly as she'd arrived. As for Love & Lace, the owner would soon see that monsters preferred to work with locals, not big corporate conglomerates using cut-throat business practices.

"Maybe they'll accept my bid," she said with enough spunk that I wanted to grin.

What was it about this tiny human that kept drawing me in? She wasn't pretty by ogre standards. In fact, most would consider her fairly ugly. But from the moment I met her at Trevor's wedding, she was all I could think—and dream—about. I spent half my nights awake with a raging hard-on and the rest of the time fuming about her surly mouth.

I wanted to kiss it. Kiss every inch of her lush body.

At Monica and Trevor's wedding, I'd hidden my lust behind snarls and the snooty demeanor that was pretty much beaten into me by my equally stiff father. Fake it until you make it, my mother always told me growing up. Do what he wants and hold onto who you were on the inside.

Lately, though, I'd begun to wonder if my snarls directed Elisa's way were holding me back.

"Where does Love & Lace come into this?" she asked, her eyes shimmering with tears.

Seeing them made something odd spark within me. I tamped the feeling down; one more skill I learned from my father.

One cannot give into urges, son, he'd said. *One must remain civilized from the moment one wakes until the moment he lays his head on his bundle roll.*

I hadn't asked what "one" might do in between, but I wondered. Could an ogre be himself inside the bedroom?

"Raze?" Elisa asked. "How is Love & Lace involved?"

"They placed their bid this morning."

"They're not from around here. Why would the fae family select them?"

"As I said, they bid low."

She frowned. "How do you know all this?"

Because I was good friends with the royal family. Ogres and elves went way back. But I wasn't going to tell

Elisa that. "Word's getting around. They rented office space at the mall."

"Damn him."

My brain locked on that one word. "*Him?*"

She huffed. "My ex runs Love & Lace. I'll bet you anything he's come here solely to drive me out of business."

"Why do something like that? From their website, Monsterville's too small for them to bother with for long."

"It's personal with him."

A growl ripped through my chest.

Elisa's eyes widened, and she reeled backward.

I coughed and banged my chest with my fist. "Indigestion."

She blinked a few times. "Okay. Anyway. He's pissed off at me and determined to see me fail at everything I do."

"Why?" I struggled to remain patient when what I wanted to do was track down her ex and rip him apart.

"I called it quits," she said. "He was getting too controlling, trying to tell me where I could go and who I could be with. I didn't like it, so I told him we were done." Her sigh bled out, and her voice went croaky with emotion. "He got mad."

I surged forward in my chair, gripping the edge of her desk hard enough a pop rang out from the wood. "He didn't hurt you, did he?"

Another snapping sound echoed in the room, and we

both stared at her desk where cracks were forming beneath my hands.

"Sorry," I said, loosening my grip. "I'll replace this, of course."

"It's okay," she said, waving it off.

When was the last time I'd destroyed someone else's property?

Never.

If I didn't know better, I'd think an ogre frenzy was settling in, but there was no ogre female around to ignite it.

My gaze fell on Elisa.

Absolutely not. She was human, incapable of igniting a frenzy in an ogre. But while I tried to shrug off the churning feeling, it persisted.

Elisa leaned forward to run her fingertip across one of the two-inch cracks. "I can sand them and put some stain on them. No one will notice after that."

I watched her finger trace the crack, and my cock surged upward, slamming against the front of my designer trousers.

Her gaze met mine, and the lust I found there was my undoing.

Rising, I swept my arm out, knocking everything off her desk. Things clattered and banged around, but all I could see was her.

She gasped, and her attention fell to the front of my pants. When her tongue dipped out to glide across her lips, I stormed around her desk, stopping beside her.

"Elisa," I growled.

She blinked up at me. "Raze?"

I pivoted her chair, so she faced me, and took her hands, tugging her up from her seat. Damn, she was tiny, the top of her head barely coming to my mid-chest. But she was lush, her body made of curves I ached to stroke.

Fire poured through me, and it would not be denied.

"I'm going to lay you on your desk," I snarled. "I'm going to lift that tight little skirt you're wearing up over your hips. I'm going to rip off your panties. Then I'm going to suck your clit and drive my tongue inside you until you come."

Her jaw dropped, and she nodded, her eyes never leaving mine.

A boost and she sat on the desk. She laid back without any further urging from me.

I dragged her body over to the edge and bunched her skirt up around her waist—she lifted her hips to make this easy for me.

A few twists of my claws, and her shredded panties dropped to the floor. I stooped down between her legs and pressed my nose against her dripping wetness, sucking in her rich honey scent.

Then I spread her thighs wider and drove my tongue inside her sweet, hot core.

CHAPTER 3

ELISA

R aze was eating me out, and I was moaning while he did it.

This morning was nothing unusual. I got up, dressed in what I called a sexy-sedate skirt and cute top, made coffee, and came to work.

Never in my wildest dreams did I imagine Raze would be doing something like this.

Thinking quickly became a difficult process.

His scratchy tongue dragged up my slit, and when he groaned, the sound hummed through my pelvic bones, lighting me on fire.

I spread my legs wider, and he munched his way up to my clit. Sucking it into his hot mouth, he nibbled on it.

I shrieked.

He lifted his head only long enough to grin. "Do that again."

The first time I saw his tusks, I inanely wondered what it would be like to kiss a guy with thumb-sized teeth projecting up from his lower jawline. Who would've thought tusks rubbing down there could feel so amazing?

His face dove between my legs again, and this time, when he sucked on my clit, he slid a finger inside me. His tail coiled up to glide across my breasts in a delicious caress.

My eyes rolling back in my head, I ground my hips up to meet him. A panting wreck, I gave into the waves rolling through me, claiming me just like this ogre was with his mouth and tongue.

He sucked harder, then released my clit to drive his tongue inside me along with his finger. He added more fingers, and the slurping, sucking sounds my body made should've made me cringe with embarrassment. Instead, I reveled in the way he made me crave him.

I clung to his horns while he sucked and licked every bit of my inside walls, his scratchy long tongue scraping across my clit each time he pulled it out.

A keen rose inside me, and it burst free. I bucked as he pumped his fingers within me, stretching me with their thick length.

His fingers went faster. My shrieks echoed around us.

He rode my body with his hand and mouth.

I let loose guttural screams as I came in one crash after another. My body shook, and I lost all control, pumping up as he sucked and swirled his tongue deep inside me.

When I finally stopped quaking, he leaned back on his haunches and grinned again.

With a nod, he rose and backed away, his gaze focused on the glistening juncture between my thighs.

I was too spent to even drag down my skirt.

"Think about my offer," he said, slowly wiping the back of his hand across his mouth. When he paused to sniff it, his nostrils flared as if he was drinking in the lingering essence of my juices.

Sparks shot through me, centering in my core, and if he stooped back down between my legs again, I'd spread them even wider.

I sensed something primal was about to rage through him. Though I couldn't imagine what it could be, heat burrowed deep within me, and I barely suppressed the urge to rise, shove him down onto my desk, then climb over him and deliver a ride to top the one he'd just given me.

Pivoting, he stalked toward the door, his gait stiff due to the pole still residing inside his pants.

He paused at the door to my office, though he didn't turn back.

He spoke normally, as if I wasn't still lying on the desk half-naked, my body still thrumming from the best orgasm I'd had in my life.

"If we combine my stellar reputation and your inge-nuity," he said in a stiff voice. He grunted. "I suspect the fae royal family will be more than happy to give us the job."

CHAPTER 4

RAZE

I was fucked. More than fucked.

Or . . . not fucked at all since my cock was still an aching rod inside my pants.

I couldn't believe what had just happened.

Elisa, a puny, irritating, totally inappropriate for me human, had ignited my mating frenzy.

Her scent lingered on my skin and in my mouth, and it was all I could do to stalk from her office and shut the door behind me.

Damn, my cock throbbed. But having sex with her would solidify my frenzy. There'd be no turning back after that.

I hobbled back to my office across from hers and sank into my chair with a groan. Propping my elbows on my desk, I held my face and stomped my feet like a child.

It isn't proper to show your emotions, my father would say. *Behave like the ogre I wish you could be.*

That was me. Always a disappointment to my father.

If I hadn't had the soft touch of my mother to soothe my wounded heart, I don't know what I would've done. Nothing my father would've liked, that was for sure.

After he died, she'd done what he would've called the unthinkable and left the ogre community, insisting I flee with her. She opened a sandwich shop in Monsterville, something else that would be a black mark according to my father. She ran her business with a silken touch that was stronger than steel. Because everyone could tell she cared about them and her product, people fought to do what she asked. If only my father had behaved in a similar manner.

Acting the way my father wanted didn't matter now that we lived among humans. They didn't care if I dressed right, held my chin up, and made sure the world never saw what I was feeling. Even here, I'd clung to the principles I'd been taught.

I'd lost all control with Elisa.

Despite his stern demeanor and the sharp smack of his hand whenever I stepped out of line, I missed my father. We'd had an uneasy relationship, mostly due to our roles within the ogre community, but there had been times when he'd patted my shoulder and told me I'd done well. When pride shone on his face.

There'd be no pride on his face now, not when I was about to bring attention to myself with this irritating frenzy.

I grumbled and stomped my feet again.

"Are you okay?" Elisa asked from the open doorway.

"I heard rumbling. I thought it was thunder at first, but the sky's clear."

"I am fine," I growled, stiffening my spine and assuming a proper pose. "I'm merely composing myself after . . ." I wrenched my mind away from the image of her splayed out before me like the most decadent feast. Of her moans while I gave her pleasure.

She studied my face, hers filled with uncertainty I didn't dare respond to. My heart urged me to cross the room and gather her into my arms. Tell her that everything would work out as it should—whatever that might be.

I'd be wise to close my business for a week or even a month and leave town. Allow my frenzy to ease off before returning. There was still time to reverse this as long as I didn't touch Elisa again.

"All right," she said, shooting me a hesitant smile. "I, um . . . yeah."

I resisted looking her way. My skin throbbed just from her voice alone, as if it stroked me, ignited me. My cock twitched, sensing she was near.

"I think we should do it," she said firmly.

"What?" I barked, my gaze shooting her way. Damn, she was lovely, a mix of an interesting face, gorgeous eyes and hair, and lush, ripe curves I wanted to sink my fingertips into. I'd tasted her wetness, and I couldn't wait to suck on her nipples. To hear her cry out as I—

No!

If I wasn't careful, my mind would lock onto her

completely and it would be over. I'd drop to my knees and beg for even a simple stroke of her hand.

At this point, I didn't even know if she liked me. Sure, she'd responded to my touch, but that could've been a whim on her part. For me, it was a burgeoning ogre frenzy built from our interactions during Monica and Trevor's wedding.

Despite her not sharing ogre beauty, I couldn't stop thinking about her from the moment I met her. My skin had tingled once when she was near. But her snappy attitude and eagerness to avoid me made it simple to dismiss the feelings gnashing around inside me.

"I meant we should combine our businesses," she said softly. "On a trial basis for the fae wedding that is. If you've changed your mind about it, however, I completely—"

"I have not." Though I should. To manage the wedding, we'd have to interact. The wedding would be enormous, involving the entire fae community. I'd be wise to let her ex take the job and stomp out of Elisa's life until my frenzy waned.

"Do you want me to move into your office?" she asked.

"No," I bit out. "Er, we can communicate by . . . text."

"Text?" Her head tilted. "Why not meet face to face?"

"I'm . . . coming down with a cold." I coughed, but it didn't sound impressive. I'd never been good at lying. Just as well I hadn't been pushed into the role my father would've insisted I take.

"I don't believe I could catch an ogre cold, could I?"

She crossed the room quickly and came right around my desk—into my inner sanctum. Before I could rise or shout for her to get away, she ran the back of her hand across my forehead. "You don't feel hot. I don't believe you have a fever." Frowning, she studied my face. I was comically bigger than her. Me sitting put us at eye-level.

When she cupped my cheeks and tipped my face this way and that, examining me, I groaned. We were so close. I could drag her into my lap and— "You don't appear sick. Maybe it's just something you ate?" Her blush rose, bringing back the flushed satisfaction that had blazed on her cheeks right after she shrieked with pleasure.

"It's not anything I ate." I'd dine on that meal every day of my life if I could.

Her rueful grin slipped out, and I appreciated her sense of humor. "Guess I shouldn't have mentioned that, right? I get the idea you'd like to pretend nothing happened in my office. I mean, I get it. You're an ogre, and I'm human."

I frowned. "Does our different species bother you?"

She shrugged. "Not a bit, but perhaps it bothers you?"

"It does not," I growled. "You're the loveliest being I've ever seen."

Her breath caught. "Thank you. You're pretty cute yourself."

"I am not cute, as you say," I bit out. "Not by what I've seen of human standards."

"I love your horns. They're so majestic." A smile

twitched across her lips. "And your tusks. I've wondered what they . . . Never mind about that."

What they . . .?

"Anyway," she said. "Don't knock yourself. It's what's inside that truly matters, and I think you're interesting, Raze."

Was interesting a good thing? It sounded like a term a female would use to let a guy down easy.

"As for the fae wedding bid, we need to get together soon to discuss it. They called after you left, asking if I had a number ready."

Her heady scent washed over me, coasting across my skin like the finest satin. Heat flared within me, a pot about to boil over.

I rose fast, knocking my chair backward. It rocked before settling.

Elisa stepped away from me with a little gasp, but the way she dragged her gaze down my front told me I hadn't scared her. Only appreciation gleamed in her eyes.

The flare of her nostrils made me wonder if humans entered a frenzy. If so, we might not be able to stop this. It would bowl over us, knocking us flat, and we'd soon be unable to keep our hands off each other.

I had to do something about this right away, but what? I'd research ogre frenzies tonight on our private ogre forum. There had to be tips there from older males, ways to circumvent what felt like something inevitable.

Having a plan made it easier to converse with Elisa in a somewhat intelligent way. "You can sit there tomorrow," I said, pointing to a chair sitting in the far corner of my fairly large office. Maybe if there was distance between us, I wouldn't catch her glorious scent. It lingered around us right now, a mix of luscious her, plus the residue of her orgasm after I ate her out. She'd enjoyed it, and she'd been quite wet.

I groaned at the memory, and flames licked across my cock, stiffening it in a flash.

"Aw, poor you. You *don't* look good. Maybe you should go home?" she said with grave concern, advancing toward me with her hand extended once more. If she touched me, I was going to shred her skirt, flip her onto my desk so I could spread her ripe ass, and impale her. "You can lie down for a bit. I'm sure you'll feel better tomorrow. I'll call the fae family back and let them know our quote will be ready within a few days. If I tell them we're bidding together, I'm sure they'll give us more time to get it ready."

"Yes, that is a wise idea." I barreled around my desk and out into the hall, only realizing then that I was fleeing *my* office. She needed to leave, not me.

"Okay, then. I'll see you tomorrow?" She passed me, heading to her own space.

I was mesmerized by her ass swaying as she walked, by how her skirt clung to her hips and thighs. She wore heels that should be impossible to walk in, yet they gave her calves a sinuous flow I found very addictive. The skirt only came to her mid-thigh, and I couldn't avoid noting her muscles flexing with her movement.

She paused in her open doorway and looked back, frowning. "Is everything okay?"

"It is," I growled. Too okay, actually.

Her lips quirked up briefly before smoothing. Turning, she sashayed into her office.

That's when I realized that unless she carried extra in her purse, she wasn't wearing panties.

My cock slammed against my trousers again.

Pivoting, I bolted for the front of the office building. I didn't stop running until I sat inside my pickup truck with the doors locked. As if that would keep my frenzy from consuming me?

Damn, I was well and truly fucked.

CHAPTER 5

ELISA

What an odd day.

An amazing day.

A puzzling day too.

That night, I sat on my sofa with my dachshund, Chickpea, curled up on my lap. I'd poured a glass of wine, and while I didn't usually drink during the week, I needed it.

"What in the world am I going to do with Raze?" I asked Chickpea. He blinked up at me and wiggled, looking extra cute with the red bow tied around his neck. "I know what I want to do with him. Oh, yeah, do I ever. But I'm not sure that jives with what he wants to do with me. He pretty much raced from his office today. You'd think I had a disease that would knock an ogre flat."

It kind of stung that he'd fled, that he'd made an excuse that he was sick—assuming that's what he'd done. I really didn't know, but he'd gone from beyond hot to chilly, which reminded me too much of how he'd behaved during Monica and Trevor's wedding weekend. As if he was drawn to me but hated the fact and would do anything he could to avoid me.

Although . . . his enthusiasm while he was licking me out today . . . His groans of pleasure . . .

Heat flared through me, pretty much shooting out the top of my head. If I kept thinking about what happened, I was going to need relief. Toys could be handy at a time like this, but for some reason, I wanted the "toy" Raze barely contained in his snug pants.

Someone knocked on my front door.

Chickpea woofed, glaring in that direction. He leaped off my lap and skittered over to the door, growling at it before spinning around and racing down the hall to my bedroom.

Shit. No.

Rising, I scooted over to stand beside the door, carefully peeking around the curtain covering the square window on the upper half.

Yup, it was Harris. Since I'd learned he was in town, I assumed I'd run into him eventually.

I could pretend I wasn't here.

"I know you're in there, Elisa," he called out. "Open the door. We need to talk."

No, we didn't. I'd said everything I needed to the last time we met. He might have things to say, but I didn't want to hear them.

"I'll break down the door if you don't open it," he said blandly.

He'd do it too. He'd studied karate for years and it

wouldn't take more than one thrust of his foot to make my flimsy lock give.

Unease prickled across my skin. I scooted down the hall and opened the bedside table drawer, removing the small gun I'd purchased when I moved here. The guy who sold it to me implied he thought I'd bought it to protect myself from monsters. He was right, but the only monster I worried about was the human kind.

I made sure it was loaded, though I left the safety on and cringed at the thought of having to use it. But I didn't trust Harris.

Back at the door, I pinched my eyes shut a second before unlocking the deadbolt and opening the door. I stepped outside before he could barge in. Shutting it wouldn't stop him, but maybe we could deal with this in public.

He looked the same. Tall, though that was relative in Monsterville. Black hair cut only by the best barbers. Jeans, a button-up shirt, and boots. The sardonic expression on his face reminded me of all the times he'd asked me where I was going, who I'd see, and then tried to pin me down to the exact time I'd return. I'd only lived with him a month before his true colors shone through.

It took six months to extract myself from his clutches. I'd cried from pent-up fury as I drove out of town for the last time. And when I settled here, I promised myself I'd never let anyone try to control me again.

"Why are you here, Harris?" I asked, keeping my weapon close to my side.

"You know why, sweetie."

"Please don't call me that." I strolled over to one of the two plastic chairs I'd placed on my tiny porch and sat.

He huffed and followed. I knew him well. He'd huffed because I'd done something without consulting him first, something as simple as taking a seat.

He dragged the second chair closer to mine and dropped into it.

I scooted my chair away from him.

A grumbled ripped from his chest, but he left his chair where it was—for now.

"I came to see if you'd come to your senses," he said.

"In what way?"

He stared at his well-manicured nails. "I expected you to come begging within a day of leaving."

I forced a chuckle. "Why would I do anything like that?"

"You need me," he growled.

"Not in the least."

"You can't run a business without me."

When I first met him, he'd impressed me with his sophistication and savvy business sense. I didn't realize until I moved in with him that his sophistication masked a stalker.

Frankly, that was why I'd been hesitant about Raze when I first met him. His well-pressed clothing and snooty demeanor reminded me too much of Harris. But by the time Monica and Trevor's weekend wedding cele-bration had ended, I'd seen past Raze's exterior to the sweet, even shy guy lurking beneath his designer suits and glasses.

"I'm actually doing quite well," I said. The nerve of Harris to suggest I couldn't succeed if he wasn't guiding my life. I stood. "You need to leave."

He latched onto my arm.

I lifted my pistol.

That got him to release me. He reeled back, his chair hitting the wall.

"What are you doing with that?" he asked.

"It's just a little precaution."

He peered around. "Monsterville. I understand."

"You're the only monster I need protection from."

"Come back to me, Elisa. I miss you." Wheedling oozed into his voice, but it was as fake as everything else about him. "We can join our businesses."

"I'm happy here in Monsterville," I said, lowering the weapon. Despite waving it around, I'd have a hard time pulling the trigger. I was more a pacifist than a warrior, though I had a spine of steel I'd back up with the steel in my hand if needed.

"If you don't come back to me, I'll ruin you again. Don't think I won't make sure no one gives you a single job."

"I can't go back with you," I said, my voice shaking. Hopefully, he didn't hear. "I've . . ." I've what? "I have a boyfriend."

"Who is it?" He glared around.

"One of the monsters living in town. He's the jealous sort. We're . . . going to move in together. You should leave before he gets here. He's got a big hammer, and he knows how to use it."

His eyes a bit wild, Harris rose and stomped over to the top step. He'd never been one to make threats unless he thought he could get away with it. At least he'd believed my boyfriend lie for now. If I was lucky, he'd be scared enough to leave town.

"I'm going to watch you," he said as he took the steps in one bound. Stopping on the walkway, he turned and glared. "You'll come running to me again, Elisa. Watch and see."

As he got into a car and drove away, I slumped in my chair.

He'd be watching. All the time.

How could I make him go away for good? Because he'd soon see I didn't have a boyfriend.

And he'd make sure I paid for lying.

CHAPTER 6

RAZE

The next morning, I should've called Elisa and told her I was still sick. Then traveled to the forest, stripped, and run off my burgeoning frenzy.

Instead, I arrived at work early with a tray of iced coffees. I didn't know what kind she liked. I also didn't know what kind of donut she preferred, so I bought three dozen, one of each they had available at Rylee's shop, Love at First Bite.

Sitting at my desk, I munched on a donut and sipped my coffee, my tail smacking the floor beside me. I pulled out the paperwork I'd prepared for the elves and studied the numbers.

"Hey," Elisa said, standing in my open doorway wearing a dark blue dress that skimmed her mid-thighs and hugged her generous curves.

Fuck, fuck. *Don't look!*

She bustled inside, shutting the door. Coming over to my desk, she grabbed the chair clients sat in and brought it around, lowering it beside mine. Her gaze fell on the boxes of donuts and iced coffee lined up on the waist-high shelf behind me. "Whoa. You must be hungry and thirsty."

"I thought you might like a donut and iced coffee. On the tray, you'll find differing flavors; they're all marked. And I asked Rylee to give us plenty of sugar, creamers, and fake sweetener. It's in the bag. As for the donuts, pick one."

"I love Rylee's baked goods. Although, I don't, um . . ." She studied the donuts, the coffee, and then me. "Thank you. No one's ever done something this nice for me before."

"Why not?" I growled.

Her eyebrows lifted. During Monica and Trevor's wedding weekend, I'd growled more than I should've. I couldn't figure out what to make of her. She was my competition, but I was strangely drawn to her.

Now I knew why.

"I don't know why no one's been nice to me." She frowned. "Don't get me wrong. My parents are great. I'm an only child, but they did everything they could to make sure I grew up happy. They've retired to Costa Rica. They live in a cute little bungalow near an inactive volcano. They go out to eat every night for dinner, go ziplining and hiking, then lounge in the hot springs spas. Did I tell you that?"

"No. Do you see them often?"

"They invite me to their home for Christmas."

"Do you go?"

She shrugged and took one of the coffees. "I have once. It's pretty there. Everyone's friendly." After placing a donut on a napkin, she sat in the chair and put her coffee and treat on my desk. Normally, I would never dream of eating in my office. It could encourage bugs. And I didn't like crumbs or powdered sugar getting on my things.

But watching Elisa sip her coffee and munch through her donut made me hungry for another. We ate in silence for a moment.

"These are amazing," she said.

"Made by an elf."

"Keebler?"

I blinked a moment. "No, one of the Loreneelis Clan works for Rylee."

She chuckled, speaking around a bite of powdered chocolate donut. "Good one."

"Yes, they are good. You can have another." I waved to the boxes.

Her head tilted. "What would you have done if I didn't like donuts?"

"Go get you a muffin?"

"Thank you, Raze."

"For what?" My face heated. Other parts of me were heating, too, but in a mellow, comfortable way. Deep inside, where my frenzy churned, I still craved her, but it was nice sitting here talking with her. Not as nice as laying her on my desk and eating her out, but it would do for now.

"Thank you for being nice. You could've been an asshole about this."

"We don't want your ex coming to our town and trying to take over."

Her lips twitched upward. "Yes, Monsterville is *our* town, isn't it?"

I gave her a nod. Feeling flustered by her smile and her lovely scent, I dragged my papers close, hunching my head over them as if I was completely absorbed in the details.

She finished her donut, sipped her coffee, and sighed. "That hit the spot."

I knew what spot I wanted to hit. I'd found it yesterday.

"I think we should offer them this." I held the papers out to her. "As you can see, they're holding the nuptials at the fae castle."

"I hope we get this job if for no other reason than that I'd love to see the fae castle."

"They've nearly completed a new castle in the mountains outside of Monsterville, but the wedding will be held at the royal family's ancestral home beyond the veil."

Her shoulders drooped. "Then I won't get to see it."

"Why do you say that? If our bid is chosen, we'll spend considerable time at the ancient castle."

"I thought humans weren't allowed there."

"Things have changed. They'll lower the veil for you to enter."

"You can go there already, can't you?" she said.

"Of course. I'm . . ." I almost named it, but when I came to the human world, I left my old life behind. I wanted to be a plain old monster like every other.

"You're what?"

"Nothing." I nudged the papers her way again. "This is a list of everything they want to include in their wedding. The vendors, naturally, will be monsters."

"Naturally."

"But they're more than willing to work with humans."

"Fortunately."

"Does the bid seem right to you? The list?"

She studied the papers. "I think so. It matches what I put together. Your bid is bold. I would've gone lower."

I scoffed. "They can afford it."

"I would've remained low to make sure my odds of getting the job were better than yours. Now, here I am, working with you to keep my ex from honing in on our business and bidding high."

"*Uneasy* partners."

"Does it have to be uneasy?"

If I was going to avoid my frenzy, yes.

"Okay, let's submit this bid," she said with a sigh. "Do you think they'll pick us?"

They would. They'd made it clear they'd prefer to work with monsters, not humans, but I wasn't going to tell her that.

"Assuming we get the job, what are we going to do about this?" She pointed to the paper in front of me. "Are we sure we can find a . . . pixie lyre quartet? That one had me stumped, though I was going to ask around if I got the bid."

"I know of a couple quartets who'd be delighted to play at the royal wedding."

"And where will we find stardust to sprinkle along the aisle?" she glanced up at me. "I was optimistic when I decided to bid, figuring I could ask Goreg or Max where to find everything on the list."

"I know where all these things can be obtained. If my mom doesn't have them, I can go to the elf apothecary."

"Where's that?"

"In town."

She frowned. "I haven't seen anything like that."

I shrugged. We might've joined the humans but anything related to the limited magic we brought with us was purposefully hidden. A human with some well-developed senses would see it, but your average person wouldn't.

"I guess it's good that you offered to work with me. Otherwise, I'd have a hard time coming up with every-thing they need." She scooted her chair closer to me.

Her heady scent hit me in the solar plexus like an orc's hammer. Stifling a groan, I moved my chair away from hers, sliding it to my left.

Frowning, she moved closer again.

I rose and dragged my chair around to the side of the desk.

She jumped up and raced around the front, heading me off before I could move my chair in that direction. Her hands smacked on her hips. "How are we going to work if you don't dare come near me?"

"Maybe I do not wish to do so."

Her lips twisted sardonically. "That wasn't an issue yesterday."

"We're going to forget that happened."

She shook her head. "No way. How am I supposed to forget an orgasm like that?"

"It was a little one."

Her snort rang out. "Not from where I was viewing it. But if you don't wish to discuss it, if you want to pretend it didn't happen, then I guess I'll go along with your wishes." She stomped around the desk and sat in her chair. "Far be it from me to ask for a repeat."

My papers dropped from my hands, fluttering to the floor. "You want me to do it again?"

She dragged the rest of the papers over to her side of the desk. "Why should I share whether I do or don't?"

"You do," I growled, my frenzy rising to the surface in a flash.

"Maybe you're right," she said with a sigh. "It was a *little* orgasm. Nothing worth discussing."

Rising, I stomped around my desk, stopping beside her. The scent of her arousal gave her away, as did the tremble of her hand on the papers.

If she kept challenging me, I'd never be able to resist her.

What *did* I want?

I wasn't sure about much, but I'd almost kill to spread her wide and lick her until she screamed again.

CHAPTER 7
ELISA

I parked my car and crossed Main Street, aiming for a new business in town called Monster Mingle. Sunlight hit the sign, making the blue-skinned minotaur emblazoned on the surface sparkle. When a gust of spring wind swept down Main Street, the sign swayed, sending me a jaunty invitation to step inside.

After what happened with Raze the other day, how could I consider going to a dating service? But with Harris stalking me and me mentioning a boyfriend, I needed a quick—preferable fake—date ASAP. If he saw me with someone else, he might give up and leave town.

My friend Paige, who'd moved to Monsterville with her fiancé, Darrow, had been after me to go to Monster Mingle for weeks now.

"You're lonely, and you said you want to meet someone new," she'd said.

I wasn't sure about that.

"Monsters make the best dating material," Paige had added.

Since she was engaged to a gorgon, she'd know.

I paused outside Monster Mingle, wondering if I was really up for making conversation with anyone on a regular basis other than Chickpea, Raze when I couldn't avoid it, and Paige.

Do it. I could almost hear Paige whispering in my ear.

After sucking in a deep breath, I tugged open the door and stepped inside. A big bell jangled overhead, and Grannie Vi came through an open doorway on the other side of the small reception area.

Her cane clunk-clunk-clunked as she hurried over to me.

"Elisa. Lovely to see you. Bub? Bub!" she called out. "We've got a customer." She latched onto my arm as if she feared I'd run—something I was seriously considering doing. "You're not lost, are you? The last two people who walked into our new business left before I could set them up with their perfect matches."

"No, I, uh . . . It's not a mistake. I came here to see what you can offer me," I said. Gulp. Harris would leave me alone if he saw me around town with a monster, right?

"Well, look who's here," Uncle Bub said, joining us, using a cane as well. Grannie Vi was about eighty, and I believed Uncle Bub was in his seventies. They'd been dating for months. "Welcome, Elisa."

She wasn't my real Grannie, and he wasn't my uncle,

but everyone called them that. She was Rylee's grand-mother and Bub was Violet's uncle.

"Haven't seen you since Monica and Trevor's wedding," Bub said. "How have you been?"

"Good." That was debatable. I mean, my skin had hummed since Raze licked me to orgasm, so one thing was positive in my life. And we might get the fae wedding job. Count that as two good things.

"You've come to Monster Mingle to be fixed up?" he asked with a toothy grin.

"I have."

Grannie was a former sex therapist. Uncle Bub was . . . well, other than baking amazing scones, I wasn't sure how he played a role in the matchmaking service, but he'd encouraged Violet to marry her gargoyle husband, Goreg, so he knew a thing or two about connecting monsters and humans.

Despite my determination, my smile slipped. For whatever reason, this felt disloyal to Raze.

He hadn't asked me out on a date.

He was behaving decently, but not like he wanted to get to know me better.

And he hadn't offered another round on my desk.

"Since my niece Violet hooked up with Goreg, a gargoyle," Bub said. "And then we fixed up Trevor and Monica; we've had a hankerin' to see who else we can help guide into wedded bliss."

"I'm not sure I'm ready to get married," I hurried to say.

"Nonsense," Grannie said, tugging me through the

doorway and down a hall. She urged me into a tiny office where she and Bub rounded a desk and sat in matching chairs. "Why else would you be here? We're not an escort service."

My eyebrows lifted.

"There's nothing wrong with that, of course," she said. "I'm all about ensuring a couple is sexually compatible in addition to what goes on outside their bedroom, but we aim to fix people up with monsters and see them walk down the aisle."

"Right you are, Elvira," Bub said, patting her hand lying on the desk. "Right you are."

"Sit, and we'll get to it," Grannie said, waving to the other chair.

My knees weak, I dropped into the seat.

"First off, I need your name," Grannie Vi said, her fingers poised over her keyboard hooked to a monitor. For whatever reason, I'd expected her to do everything on paper. I should've realized that even the elderly would be computer savvy.

She and Bub went through the basic information before getting to the nitty gritty stuff.

"Sexual preference?" Vi asked, not looking away from her screen.

"Male."

"What do you enjoy?"

I frowned. "You mean kinks and stuff like that?"

"If you're willing to share."

Bub turned to stare out the window behind them as if that would put me at ease.

"I, um, like big cocks," I gasped out.

"Don't we all, love," Grannie said with a wink. "Don't we all."

"And big guys, which fits with monsters." Why couldn't I stop thinking of one particular ogre? I should shove his gorgeous green eyes hiding behind his glasses from my mind. And his broad shoulders. His narrow waist. His cute ass.

Really, I had it bad for Raze, the too-snooty, uptight, sneering ogre I'd been crushing on since I met him.

"I'll note big all around," Grannie said. "Do you wish to have children?"

"Yes."

"Allergies?"

I frowned. "I throw up seafood. Is that what you mean?"

"I was referring to fur. We already had one match fail because yetis shed. Did you know that? They're not hypoallergenic."

"I'm not allergic to fur."

"Very good." She tapped away on her keyboard. "Tentacles?"

"What about them?"

"Are you open to suction?"

"Oh, my, I suppose so," I said, trying to picture exactly what she might mean. Ah, yes, I got it. Heat climbed into my face.

"What's your idea of a daring date?" she asked.

"Something I'd like to do or something I wouldn't?" This was more complicated than I thought it would be.

"Something you'd find exciting to do on a date with a monster."

"Hmm." I nibbled on my lower lip. "I enjoy experiencing new cultures. It might be fun to visit with his monster friends or family and get to know them."

"Alright." She asked me a few, though more mundane questions, then tapped a few buttons. A ping rang out and the printer sitting on a table to her left hummed. "It looks like we have a match already." She clapped her hands, and her eyes gleamed. "How wonderful!"

"So quickly?" I asked.

"We have quite a database of monsters eager to get to know humans. It's been a bit more challenging getting the humans to sign up for our service, but seeing Violet happy with Goreg, plus Storm, the wolf shifter, and his human love, Luna, getting engaged has driven up the interest. I'm still unsure how things will work out with . . . I guess I should remain confidential about other clients."

I frowned. "Like whom?"

"Oh, you know." Leaning forward, she lowered her voice to a very loud whisper. "We have elf customers, a phoenix, and I'm trying to rope in our local demon."

I gulped. "Demon?"

"Sheriff Venom. He might be a grump on the surface, but I'm sure there's a heart of gold beneath his burnished bronze skin. Those broad horns arching up over his head! A girl could latch onto them during intimate moments, don't you think?"

I hadn't heard we had a demon sheriff in town. I suppose if anyone could keep order, it would be a demon.

"As for the elf," her head tilted, "you did say you're interested in having babies."

"Not right now."

"Hmm." She wrangled her lower lip with her dentures. "If you were open to marrying immediately, I'd fix you up with an elf with royal connections. He needs a bride quick, and he's determined to have it."

"I'm only interested in dating at this time."

Her gaze lifted to the open door behind me, and I turned.

"There he is now." She half rose. "Come on in, Tylik. I was just telling Elisa about you."

"Elisa?" The most gorgeous male I'd ever seen remained in the doorway. I gaped, taking in his tall, muscular frame. He'd pulled up some of his long golden hair into a man bun at the back of his head, leaving the rest draping around his shoulders. Talk about droolworthy. The arrangement exposed his pointed ears. I'd stepped into a fantasy movie, and he was the star.

He strolled toward me, his hand extended and a sultry smile on his lips.

"Elisa here is looking for a date," Grannie said. "Tylik is looking for an immediate wife. Seems like a match made in heaven."

"You're so right, Vi," Uncle Bub said.

"I don't want to have to get married," I shouted, yanking

back the hand I'd extended toward him. While I was at it, I wrenched my gaze from his. I'd heard that elves could lure a person in. They wouldn't let you go until they were finished with you, and that could take ages. Although, I'd also heard elf magic was pretty much nonexistent beyond the realm.

"It is . . . very nice to meet you." Tylik backed away, his eyes widening.

"Alright then," Grannie said. She waved toward Tylik. "She said no, and we will not try to talk her into anything she's not comfortable with. Win some, lose some, I always say, Tylik. If you'll wait in the lobby, I'll finish with Elisa, and we can see what my database has churned up for you."

He bowed. "Thank you, my lady."

Grannie simpered. "I just love how he calls me that and all the fancy words he uses." She tapped Bub's shoulder. "Take a cue, my man. Take a cue."

"I will wait in the vestibule until you can attend to me." Pivoting, he strode down the hall.

Turning to the printer, Grannie Vi lifted a piece of paper and squinted at it. "Good thing we have a back-up plan for you, Elisa. Friday night. Dinner at the Horny Café, seven sharp."

"Horny . . .?"

Her cackle rang out. "Monsters run it. Horns. Horny. Get it? Love that name."

"Oh, yeah, sure," I said, shaking my head. "Where is it located?"

She gave me the address.

"And my date's name?" Maybe I could bribe him to pretend to be my boyfriend for a week or so.

"Now that's the fun part about Monster Mingle," Bub said, his big grin revealing his pristine, white teeth. "His name's a surprise. When you get to the restaurant, mention us, and they'll take you to your table. He'll be waiting."

"Alright. How much do I owe you?" I held out my debit card.

"Not a thing," Grannie said. "We're doing this because it's fun; not to make money off monsters and humans finding true love together."

"That's sweet of you."

"And when you and your match decide to join in wedded bliss," she said, waving to a row of pink bags sitting on a high table along one wall, "Come back and get your honeymoon package from us." She leaned forward, and while she lowered her voice, it still came through loud and clear. "We've got some sex toys in there."

I wasn't sure my face could get much hotter, but I also wasn't surprised. Grannie Vi had a reputation for giving creative gifts.

"Thank you," I said, rising.

"You're very welcome," Bub said. "Let us know how your date turns out."

"I will."

On Friday night, I pulled my car into the parking lot of the Horny Café. While my engine ticked down, I took in the enormous horns mounted above the main entrance. What kind of creature had they come from? Last I knew, wooly mammoths were extinct.

Maybe coming here was a big mistake. I hadn't seen Harris since he made his threat, and we were supposed to hear about our bid on the fae wedding within a week. As far as I could tell, he hadn't bid on anything else.

If Harris didn't get the fae wedding, he might give up and slink out of town.

I wouldn't want to get a monster's hopes up tonight, because I was really only looking for a pretend boyfriend.

Deciding I might as well go meet him, I left my car. Inside, I mentioned Grannie Vi and Uncle Bub, and told the griffin host my name and followed the half-lion, half-eagle's padding footsteps through the main room and onto the glassed-in deck looking out across the valley and the snow-tipped mountains beyond.

"Right here," the griffin said, waving to my date with the tip of one of his wings.

I came to a halt.

Ugh. No.

Raze scowled at me from where he sat at the table for two.

CHAPTER 8
RAZE

I was only at the Horny Café because Darrow had talked me into going to Monster Mingle. And because I'd thought going out with someone would help me get over the frenzy brought on by Elisa.

My skin started tingling a few seconds ago. I should've known she was near.

When I saw her following the griffin over to my table, my cock started knocking on my pants.

The griffin grinned my way. "Your date for the evening." When he shot Elisa a leer, I growled. His huff rang out, and he lifted off, flying over the guests and back to the podium near the front door.

"I, um . . ." Elisa said, her hands fidgeting at her sides. She wore a pretty green dress and heels that went on for miles. She'd swept her hair up, and she was the prettiest person I'd ever seen.

I couldn't read her feelings from her somewhat stunned expression.

"Did you do something to make this happen?" she asked.

Because her question didn't come out like an accusation, I didn't snap. "No, but I assume Grannie Vi and Bub are having a laugh right about now."

"But they tried to fix me up with an elf who's looking for someone to walk down the aisle with him immediately."

"What?" I barked.

She flicked her hand out. "I turned Tylik down."

Tylik? He'd only been in town about a month. From what I'd heard, he'd had a home built, helping with the construction, but he'd barely moved out of the elf embassy.

Why was he looking for someone to marry him so suddenly?

It was all I could do not to demand she tell me more. She owed me nothing, however, and what Tylik wanted was none of my business unless it applied to Elisa.

"Grannie Vi and Uncle Bub know we don't get along," she said. "They were at Monica and Trevor's wedding. They saw us snarling at each other all the time."

"We've gotten along okay this past week," I said, scratching the back of my neck. I yanked on my collar, loosening my tie.

She shifted from one hip to the other. She hadn't sat. Did that mean she was rejecting this farce of a date?

Hell, maybe she was reconsidering taking Tylik up on his bride-making offer.

I wrenched on my hair and then my tie again.

"Have you ever thought of taking it off?" she asked with a frown.

"Excuse me?" I asked, blinking up at her. I could picture sweeping everything off this table, stripping her —and myself—fast, and showing her that yes, I could take it all off. My cock shouted that it was up for something like that.

"I meant your tie," she said with a laugh. Pulling out the chair opposite me, she sat. "Since I'm here, we might as well have dinner." Her breath caught. "Unless you'd rather not dine with me. We pretty much share an office. That might be enough "us" time for you already."

"Please stay." Even I could hear the humble tone in my voice.

I was beginning to think there would never be enough alone time for us. Was I falling for Elisa?

Yes.

My frenzy might be driving me, but I'd been attracted to her from the second I saw her before Trevor's wedding.

So now I felt my heart and soul sinking into the abyss called Raze's frenzy, and I held open my arms to take her with me. Elisa made me laugh. And I craved her.

"As for the tie, I'm not sure what I'd do without clothing like this." I flicked the front of my suit.

"You must wear something more comfortable when you're at home." Her laugh rang out again before I could answer. "Actually, I used to picture you sitting on a deck or in your living room still dressed in a suit."

She wasn't far off.

"My father always told me it was important to present the right image." That was putting it lightly. My father would've chastised me if I hadn't.

"Even when you're at home? That's when you should be able to relax and let loose. Do you wear shorts?"

"Shorts?"

"You know, cut off pants."

"And bare my legs?"

She snickered. "What, are they hairy?"

"What if they are? And knobby."

Her shoulders lifted. "It's you and there's nothing wrong with a few bumps and patches of hair."

Was there even a smidgen of a chance she liked me?

I'd come here only half-heartedly, feeling like I should make an effort to go out with someone, maybe break the frenzy by being with someone different. But all I wanted was to be with Elisa.

Whenever she looked at me, sure, my cock noticed and responded, but I liked being with her. She was funny and clever and incredibly sexy. Her soul touched mine in a way no one else's ever had.

"You must be thinking about something serious, Raze," she said, tapping a fork on the table.

"Why?"

"Your face is scrunched. I can leave if you want. I imagine you'd rather spend your personal time with anyone but me."

I leaned forward, bracing my arms on the table. "What if I *do* want to spend my personal time with you?"

CHAPTER 9
ELISA

I gulped. "Really?"

When Raze smiled, I heard music. Imaginary butterflies danced around my head. My heart caught a big wave and rode it all the way to shore.

Tusks were incredibly sexy.

"Really," he said softly. "I keep thinking about the fun we had together during Monica and Trevor's wedding weekend."

"You mean like when you chastised me for trying to work on our joint ice sculpture with a chainsaw?" I followed my comment up with a grin. Looking back, I could laugh. Then? Not so much.

Things had changed.

He laughed, a boisterous, amazing sound that drew the attention of everyone in the room, maybe because it was so unexpected from a guy who came across as stiff and snooty.

It was infectious. I joined in, speaking through my

chuckles. "And then when we went on the sleigh ride, I kind of accidentally spilled my mulled wine on your suit." It truly had been an accident, though he'd accused me of doing it on purpose.

"Despite the mishaps, I enjoyed being with you."

I studied his face. "Are you saying that to be kind?"

"Didn't you have fun too?"

I had. Too much, which was why it hurt when he kept rejecting me. "Why are we able to communicate now when we couldn't then?"

He shrugged. "Maybe this setting works better?"

Maybe.

"Can I get you something to drink?" a troll server asked. She'd dyed her hair bright yellow, and the dress she wore brought out the blue of her eyes. She grinned from me to Raze. "And welcome. I don't believe I've seen either of you at the Horny Café before."

We shook our heads.

"Would you like wine or something different to drink?" Raze asked me.

"I'd love some wine. White or red works for me."

He studied the wine list and tilted it the troll's way, pointing.

"Very well, sir," she said. "Fine choice." She shot me a sweet smile before zipping toward the kitchen.

We studied our menus, and I chuckled at some of the selections. This place definitely catered to monsters.

"Dragon-fried filet?" I said with a snort.

He frowned, looking serious, though his lips

twitched, and his gorgeous green eyes sparkled behind his glasses. "You haven't had it before?"

"Nope."

"Dragon fire gives the filet the perfect flavor. A hint of smoke and the essence of magic."

"Do dragons actually exist other than Vrok's dragonettes?" Which only looked like dragons. "I thought dragons were a myth."

"No more a myth than ogres."

"I guess you're right." I studied the menu further. "Vampire bites. Ha."

His gaze focused on my neck. "Do you enjoy bites?"

With his tusks? My bones softened as lust swirled through me. Definitely yes.

"I'd have to try it to find out," I said, feeling very bold. "Do you think there's anyone around who'd be willing to offer a nibble?"

His eyes widened.

Maybe he didn't hate me after all?

He gulped. Was he regretting his teasing offer already?

Worried that he was, I studied the menu some more. "Ghoul-ash. Mummy wrap. I'm going to pass on the brain-in-a-bun, however."

"Some of the choices are just cute names. I don't believe they actually serve brains, though I've heard selkies enjoy them."

"There really are selkies?"

"They're as real as ogres and dragons," he said with a grin. "As for bites . . ."

He wasn't going to let that go, was he? I leaned forward as excitement soared through me. He's done some fancy tongue work between my legs, but he'd yet to kiss my mouth. I wanted to taste him, feel him.

He shifted toward me.

I scooted closer. Our breaths mingled. He smelled good, a mix of wildflowers and wood smoke with a hint of musk and a dash of adventure. Everything wrapped up in a gorgeous ogre body. The air around us carried the mystery of the unknown and the excitement of endless possibility.

"Elisa," he groaned.

"Raze." My whisper was full of the longing for something I couldn't define, something I sensed only Raze could give me.

The moment was at hand, and this could change everything. We'd soon—

"So, is this your boyfriend?"

Ugh. I flopped back in my chair, staring up at Harris, who stood beside the table glaring from me to Raze.

"This is Raze," I said. "Raze? This is my slimy ex who undercut all my prices until my business failed."

Raze growled and stood, towering over Harris.

Harris had the sense to back a few steps away. Color flooded his face, and he rallied, stomping right up to Raze. "Elisa's mine. If you think I'll hand her over to a monster like you, you've got another think coming."

I scrambled out of my chair. "Go away, Harris."

"Elisa belongs to herself." Death came through in Raze's voice. Couldn't Harris hear it?

I'd say not.

He grabbed onto the lapels of Raze's jacket and shook him—or tried to. Raze remained as solid as a stone wall, glaring down at Harris.

"Your relationship is over," Harris snarled. "I'm taking Elisa where I can show her who's boss." He released Raze. Latching onto my arm, he started hauling me toward the entrance.

Anger bolted through me. How dare he come here and try to grab me? I reeled backward, wrenching away from his grip.

Raze stormed over, thrusting himself between us.

"Do you want to be with this asshole?" he asked me.

"Absolutely not." My voice shook. I hated how my old life kept trying to stomp on my new one. And I hated Harris.

Raze gave me a feral grin. "Why don't I show him how your *boyfriend* treats someone trying to harm his girlfriend?"

He grabbed Harris by the scruff of his neck, lifted him off the floor, and shook him until Harris's teeth rattled.

CHAPTER 10

RAZE

Could I get away with killing the male who'd dared touch Elisa?

"I will rip your head off and stomp it beneath my shoe," I snarled. I whipped my tail up and coiled it around his throat. Not too tight, but enough to show him I meant business.

Harris made some high-pitched sounds and chopped at my arms, his eyes widening when I didn't flinch. His leg kicked out fast and probably brutal when it hit a human. Again, I didn't flinch.

"Stop," Elisa cried, wedging herself between us before I could rearrange Harris's nose.

I released the jerk, and he tumbled to the floor. Rising, he rubbed his ass and glared.

"Get out of here, Harris," Elisa sputtered, pointing toward the door. "Leave me alone. I never want to see you again."

He straightened his clothing, stiffening. "This monster just assaulted me."

"Then I've arrived at just the right time," someone snarled behind us. "Allow me to introduce myself. I'm the local sheriff."

Harris gulped, staring at the tall, broad demon with skin the color of flames, horns, and a fiery gleam in his dark eyes who strode forward to join us. "What in the hell are you?"

"Exactly," Venom said with a slick grin.

"Allow me to introduce Monsterville's sheriff," I said.

Venom's gaze landed on me. "Why did you touch him?"

"Because he dared to lay his hands on her."

"He assaulted me," Harris cried, flinging his arms out. "He attacked me for no reason, hauling me off my feet and shaking me."

"He grabbed my arm and tried to make me leave with him," Elisa said, her voice shaking. "He hit Raze and kicked him. Harris knows karate, and he used those moves on Raze."

I wanted to leap over Venom and take Harris to the ground. Show him how ogres treated the females they . . .

I didn't love Elisa, but I could. If anyone tried to harm her, I'd shred them.

"Did you want to leave with him?" Venom asked Elisa.

"Absolutely not. He's my ex-boyfriend, and I've told him to leave me alone numerous times."

Venom growled. My snarl joined in.

Harris's eyes widened. "Elisa is—*was*—mine," he said stiffly. "I have every right to speak with her. This is public property—"

"A restaurant is private property," Venom said.

"Whatever," Harris said. "I want to press charges. He assaulted me, and as sheriff, you need to arrest him."

Venom tapped Elisa's arm. "Do you want to press charges? You say he grabbed you."

"I will if he does," Elisa said. "What's it going to be, Harris? If you press charges, so will I."

"How can you want to be with a . . ." Harris's sneer traveled down my front. "I don't even know what this abomination is."

"I'm an ogre," I said. "The ogre who will peel your skin from your body if you touch my girlfriend again."

"I like that, Raze," Venom said with a grin. "I'd do the same thing. Protecting a friend is one of the most vital things anyone can do. If I'd done the same . . ." He shook his head. "The past doesn't matter." His deadly gaze hit Harris. "Are you pressing charges or not?"

Harris shifted his neck, tugging on his shirt. "I didn't do anything wrong."

"You touched my girlfriend," I said. "Do it again, and we won't be having a discussion."

Elisa's wide eyes met mine. She'd heard me back up the boyfriend claim. We weren't dating, of course, but if she had a reason to say we were, I would support her.

I held out my hand to her, and when she took it, I tugged her close, tucking her into my side. She felt right there, as if she should stay there forever.

My frenzy still simmered within me, but what I felt now was different. Yes, I wanted her, but I wasn't only driven by the mating lust inside me. I'd wanted her from the moment I met her. *Her*, not just sex.

Venom flicked a claw toward Harris, lifting the male off the floor. "You have not given me an answer."

"No charges," Harris cried in a strangled voice.

Venom dropped him, and he landed hard on the floor.

"Leave," Venom told him. "Do not go near Elisa again."

A pop, and Venom disappeared.

"You're not welcome here," our troll server said, stomping up to Harris. She pointed to the door. "Go. Do not return."

"Don't think this is over, Elisa," Harris snarled.

When I growled and stepped toward him, he squeaked. Pivoting fast, he bolted for the door.

"Well," Elisa said with a heavy sigh.

I took her hand and squeezed it, wishing I could take us back to joking about the menu. "Would you like to leave?"

She shook her head. "I want to have dinner with you."

My heart flipped over. "Then let's sit back down."

"Right," our server said, bustling over with a bottle of wine. "Let me get this poured, and then I'll take your meal orders."

After she left, Elisa leaned forward, keeping her voice low. "I didn't mean to imply you were my boyfriend.

When Harris came to my apartment the other day, it slipped out, though I didn't name anyone. That's why I went to Monster Mingle; to find a fake boyfriend. I won't hold you to this."

I could back away like I'd done from each of her overtures during Trevor's wedding weekend, or I could grab onto the best offer in my life. "What if I want you to hold me to it?"

CHAPTER 11

ELISA

"You want a fake girlfriend?" I asked, needing to clarify this.

"I find myself in need of one. Unless you're withdrawing your offer, that is."

I slumped in my chair, stunned, and he took the seat opposite mine. "You don't like me."

"I think we've already established that isn't true."

"Then you do like me?" When he hesitated, I held up my hand. "No need to answer that. Sorry. I'm pushing again." I frowned. "Wait. You said you *need* a girlfriend?"

"Er, yes," he said, his gaze sliding away from mine. "I have an upcoming engagement and if I don't bring a potential mate, my family will bring out one female after another, demanding I pick one."

"You might meet someone you like from among them." I had to point that out. Someone he'd rather date than me.

"What if I already have?"

Oh, shit. He liked someone? "Then take her?"

He rolled his eyes. "Elisa. I'm speaking of you."

"Back off here for a second. I told Harris I was engaged. I went to Monster Mingle hoping to meet someone who I could pretend was my boyfriend if Harris saw us around town. You're the guy they fixed me up with. Harris arrived and made the assumption I thought he would, though I didn't expect him to attack you."

"You said you went to Monster Mingle to find a fake boyfriend?"

"I also wanted to . . ." Best not to mention that I hoped I could find someone who'd make me forget how much I liked Raze. There was no chance of that. "Anyway. Harris made assumptions, and you jumped in like a hero to back me up. But now that I'm giving you a way out, you're suggesting you want to continue pretending we're dating?"

"Not suggesting, asking."

"You need a girlfriend for a family engagement. I could do that for you anyway."

"If you don't want to be my real pretend girlfriend, just say so." His words came out stoic, but I was beginning to learn Raze's starched exterior hid a big soft heart.

"I don't mind."

"Way to make a guy feel good," he said with a laugh.

"Are you sure about this, Raze?"

His eyes met mine, and for the first time, I felt like I saw the true Raze, a nice guy who was as lonely as me. "Completely."

I reached across the table. "Then we have a deal."

"We do." He took my hand and kissed it.

CHAPTER 12

RAZE

"I need you to organize a family gathering," I told my mom at her sandwich shop, Monstrous Munchies, the next day.

"Hand me those peppers, would you?" She pointed her knife at the colored vegetables sitting on the counter to my left, and I gave them to her. "And take off that infernal jacket."

I blinked down at my suit. "It's important that I look my best."

"Raze. Honey." She cupped my cheeks, nearly stabbing me in the left eyeball with her blade when she squeezed them. "I should've left your father before you could walk."

"He wouldn't have allowed it." Their marriage had been arranged by their families. The entire ogre community would've been horrified if she'd left him.

"Still should've. I could've taken you far away from his strict influence."

"He wasn't that bad." Despite giving into his temper too often. "He did the best he could with me." Only hitting me once when he thought I wasn't presenting a good enough impression.

"I should've killed him, then," she said, her grim gaze meeting mine. She knew exactly what I was remembering.

"They would've killed you just as quickly." Then I'd have no one. I would've survived. My father's heavy discipline had made sure I could handle almost anything. But the loss of my mother would've wrecked me.

"You understand what I'm saying. Have you considered doing a cleansing to rid yourself of your father's lingering presence?"

"Do you think the ancient ogre ritual will drive him from my mind?" I was skeptical.

She shrugged. "It can't hurt to try, can it? Ogres are ancient ones. We lived in the days of magic."

"All of that's within the veil now, in the elf and fae realms."

"I like to think we brought a little bit of our magic with us."

I hadn't felt it, but I guess that didn't mean it didn't exist. "Maybe. I don't know. I'll think about it."

"I understand. Look at me." Her low chuckle ranging out, making her gorgeous, golden ogre body shake. "Here I am suggesting you let go of your past and embrace the world we now live in, then suggest you perform a cleansing."

"This is our life now."

"You're right." Her gaze took in her apron with the shop's name emblazoned on the front, and she poked at the hair net holding her long dark hair tight on the top of her head. "Who would've thought I'd be chopping my own vegetables, let alone running a sandwich shop?"

"You would've laughed at the thought." I would've, too, for that matter. "You would've looked down your nose at me and fingered your favorite tiara, stating you would only touch something like that to bring it to your mouth."

"That's right." Her smile told me she wasn't sad about leaving the trappings of our prior life behind, though her tone came out wistful. "I miss that tiara sometimes. The foot massages too."

"I will massage your feet whenever you wish."

She snorted. "Maybe I want a cute ogre—a few years older than you, I should add—doing it instead of my sweet son."

I cocked my head. "You've considered dating?" My father had been gone for five years. It made sense she'd want to spend her life with someone new.

"Why not?" Her challenge rang out.

"There's a new matchmaking service in town, Monster Mingle. I imagine they can fix you up on a few dates."

"Do you think they offer ogres?"

"I'm an ogre and I went there."

"Maybe I'd like to date a gargoyle." She sighed. "Those wings. And that lovely steely gray color to their skin. I could almost eat them u—" She coughed. "You know what I mean."

I did. I felt the same way about Elisa, like I wanted to eat her up—again. I would never mention that to my mother, however.

"I'll think about it." She nudged her chin in my direction. "Take off the jacket. Live a little." She carefully sliced the top and bottom off an onion, then made razor-thin cuts along one side, scooping up the slices and placing them in a plastic bin. Like some of the big chain sandwich shops, she made meals to order, using only the freshest cuts of meat from the town's centaur butcher, plus vegetables grown by sprites. "Roll up your sleeves while you're at it and get to work."

"You wish for me to bare my arms?" I asked, almost shocked. Removing my jacket was one thing. And contrary to Elisa's chuckling comment, I did remove my jacket when I sat inside my home. Sometimes even my tie!

"Raze. *Honey.*" Mom's smile told me she knew she was repeating herself. "We're part of the human world now. We joined them by choice, but surely you're finding you enjoy the path our lives have taken."

I thought of Elisa. "Definitely."

"Then ditch the suit. Bare your arms. Wear . . . I don't know. Shorts maybe? It's warmed up nicely. You've got decent legs."

My laugh snorted out. "I do have nice legs."

"*Decent*, I said. Decent." She kept her focus on the vegetables she was chopping, but her smile rose even further. I'd seen my mother smile more since coming to the human world than in all the years we'd spent among ogres. "Get chopping." She poked a second cutting board and knife laying on the counter in front of me. "And tell me why we suddenly need to hold a family gathering."

"I have a girlfriend."

"Ah!" she tossed the knife aside, impaling the wall—on purpose, as she was deadly with knifes. She leapt at me, nearly knocking me over. Ogre females were often as big and brawny as males, something we took pride in. My mother was nearly my height. "A girlfriend! Who's the lucky female? Or male! Never doubt I accept you no matter who you wish to be with. Love is love, though you did say girl."

"Her name's Elisa. And here's the thing. We're not really actually dating. We're *pretending* to date."

Mom backed up to lean against the counter, frowning while I explained about Elisa's ex.

"Just kill him and get it over with," she said.

"I would like to kill him," I admitted. "But you're the one who said we need to fit in with humans. They don't —usually—kill others."

"Eh, Venom will let something like that slip. You said he threatened her. That's a good enough reason to kill him." Easing away from me, she wrenched her knife from the wall and swept it through the air. "If you're squeamish about it, I'll do it for you."

"Please, Mom. No." I grunted. "We need to fit in not only in regards to clothing."

"I suppose." Her lips twisted. "Are you sure about not

taking care of the matter? I could slice his head off with one blow."

I'd seen her do it, back in the days when a mealy ogre duke threatened me. One swipe, and he was no longer coming after little boys.

"Let me handle this."

She huffed and lowered the knife. "Don't think I won't seek him out and show him he's making a huge mistake challenging our family." She tossed the knife aside and wrapped her arm around me. "Tell me more about your lovely girlfriend."

"Pretend girlfriend."

"She'll see how wonderful my son is and wish to make this permanent."

If only. It was a dream for me.

"Elisa's amazing." I couldn't stop grinning. "She's about this tall." I made a chopping motion at my mid-chest. "She's sweet and smart, and she makes me laugh."

"*Why* the fake girlfriend, then?" Mom asked. "I want a real daughter. Maybe have a pretend engagement followed by a pretend wedding only really take her to bed. I want little ogres—half—scampering about. You like her. I can tell you want to be with her. Toss her over your shoulder and take her into the woods. Show her what you can offer in the ancient ogre way."

Ogres used to claim their mates. Since females were so gloriously brawny, the male often had to battle the female and defeat her before she would permit him to touch her. It fired a male's blood.

My frenzied blood was fiery enough already.

"We can't do that with humans," I said. "They wish to be courted. Wooed politely."

Her face scrunched. "Humans have too many strange customs. Like the holiday where they dress up as monsters."

"Halloween."

"Yes, that one. Ogres would never go from one house to another, begging. Or the April holiday where they expect rabbits—a food source, for fate's sake—to bring them chocolate." She frowned. "I do adore chocolate, however. That's one human thing I would not wish to live without."

"I don't understand Easter, but I do like Christmas."

"The songs! And the tree. I plan to decorate one this coming season even if it means I must bring large foliage into my home."

"I'll help you. We can go into the woods and cut one down together."

"Perhaps you and Elisa will wish to do this by yourselves," she said slyly.

I doubted we'd still be together by Christmas. Assuming we were awarded the bid, the fae wedding would be long past, and I or my mother would've eliminated the threat of Elisa's former boyfriend.

"Perhaps," I said.

"As for a family gathering," she said. "I believe I can put something together. How soon?"

"Not too soon."

"This weekend. I wish to meet her."

"That's too soon."

"Surely my wonderful son can convince her to make this real over the next four days."

"I'll try," I said valiantly.

"Then we'll hold the Ogre Games, complete with competitions and . . ." She grinned slyly. "You can take a steam bath afterward with your *real* fiancée."

CHAPTER 13

ELISA

"Hey!" My new friend, Luna, stood in the open doorway to my office, holding hands with Storm, her wolf shifter fiancé. "We have an appointment?"

"Yes, come in," I said. "Let me grab Raze." The words came out much too easily. When they'd called to set up an appointment, Luna hesitantly asked if Raze and I could co-coordinate their wedding. I'd said yes we were partners, but leaving out that the partnership might end sooner than I'd like.

But we had his family event this weekend. Some sort of ogre event, and he'd mentioned a steaming pool. I think. He told me to bring a bathing suit.

"I'll be right back," I told Storm and Luna. "Have a seat." As they dropped into chairs, I hurried to the office across from mine, pausing in the doorway. Raze didn't notice me, and I watched as he stared down at his desk as if his life couldn't get more wretched. It made my heart pinch tight.

Entering his office, I shut the door and walked over to his desk. When I touched his shoulder, he looked at me with a jerk of his head.

"Ah, Elisa," he said. "You . . ." His gaze fell on my mouth, and for the thousandth time, I wondered what it would be like to kiss him. We'd been more intimate already than some married couples, yet I didn't know what he tasted like.

As if he heard my thoughts, he groaned. He rose so fast, his chair shot backward. Lifting me off my feet, he stomped over to the wall and pressed me against it, stepping between my widespread thighs, thrusting his body against mine.

He growled, and his head lowered. "I'm going to kiss you, Elisa."

The last time he made demands like this, I was so stunned, I couldn't speak. It was all I could do to think. I'd only wanted to feel.

"You'd better," I said decisively.

He blinked behind his glasses. "Do you mean that?" A hint of vulnerability came through in his voice. Didn't he realize I wanted him? I suppose I hadn't told him. I'd get to that soon. Lips were all that mattered right now.

"I mean it," I growled. "Kiss me!"

His lips twitched up on one side before he pressed his mouth against mine. He was gentle at first, but the sparks flinging themselves around inside me wanted more.

I wanted more.

I clung, pulling him tighter against me and heaven help me, but I ground my pussy against him.

He shifted himself upward, rubbing his stiff cock into the juncture between my thighs. It was big. I wanted to feel it moving inside me. But how could I do that through clothing? The thought of ripping his suit off him had merit, but I was too focused on the feel of it dragging up my slit and hitting my clit.

With his tail coiled around my waist, holding me in place, I rode him, keening and whimpering, clutching his shoulders. His tongue plunged inside my mouth and his glorious cock rubbed me into complete madness.

I came all at once, a damn let loose, everything inside me shattering.

With a growl, he joined me, groaning as he jerked against me a few more times, his cock wrenching upward.

CHAPTER 14
RAZE

I'd just humped my not-girlfriend against the wall of my office. Anyone could step inside the room and see us, and I hadn't given a damn.

My father would smack me if he could hear my thoughts.

But he was dead, and I was my own male now. I decided what I did and did not do with my life. Perhaps my mother was right. I needed to try to put my father's heavy presence behind me.

Elisa watched me, though. Did I see disappointment in her eyes?

I must.

"I apologize," I groaned, pressing my forehead against hers. My frenzy might be sated for this moment, but already, my cock sensed her nearness and twitched, eager to explore more of her body.

My frenzy would keep building in waves, and it

would be all I could do to keep my hands off her when I crested each peak.

"Are you saying you're sorry we did that?" she asked in a tiny voice.

Hold on.

It hit me all at once. She wasn't disappointed. She thought *I* was upset it happened. Communication was a tough thing; I needed to learn how to do it better. With my father, silence and agreement had always been the right answer, but I refused to let my father rule my behavior from the grave.

Hearing her vulnerability wrenched my soul sideways. "I'm only sorry if you are."

She frowned. "I'm not sorry it happened, Raze. I enjoyed it."

"You did?" I hated that I sounded incredulous.

She nodded, a smile teasing across her lips.

"Why?" I asked.

When she wiggled, I lowered her to the floor, and she stepped out of my embrace and beneath my arm. "Because you and I—"

"Hey, do you guys want us to come back another time?" Luna asked from the hall. "There was some banging going on. Are they working on the roof or something?"

No, but I'd just worked on me and Elisa.

"We should go to my office," she said, her cheeks bright red and her pretty skirt and sweater rumpled. I'd done that, and I was eager to rumple her some more. I also wanted to ask her what she'd been about to say, but now wasn't the time. There may never be a time.

"Raze?" she asked.

"What?"

"Do you want me to talk to them by myself, or can you come with me?"

"Oh, I'll go with you."

Her gaze fell on the front of my pants. "Oh, my."

I glanced down, sighing when I took in how wet I was. "Ogres have lots of cum."

Her breath caught. "Oh, really?" She sounded more intrigued than disgusted, but I had to be reading her wrong. No one enjoyed lots of cum. Well, I didn't mind it. Some ogres were quite proud of how much they could produce. I'd never really thought much about it.

"Some even say it tastes good." Shit. Why had I said that?

"Like, sweet or salty or spicy?"

I frowned. "I'm not sure. I haven't tried mine."

She shrugged. "Some guys would."

Would *she*? I could hear my father's stern voice in my head. It would be impolite—*improper*—to ask, and it was important that a male of my lineage always behave in the most civilized manner.

Damn, I wished I could kick him from my mind.

"We could . . . tie a shirt around your waist." Her grin slipped out. "Sorry?"

"Never be sorry for that."

"Oh, I'm not." She said it decisively, as if she truly meant it. But she couldn't. This was fake.

Or was it?

Now I couldn't wait for the weekend and the steam bath. Maybe it was time I acted like a true ogre and claimed my mate.

"I'll do this," I said, unbuttoning my jacket and draping it over my arm so it hung in front of the evidence. "Will this do?"

She nodded. Stepping forward, she stroked along my jaw. "Later, I want you to tell me more about your cum."

ELISA

Flavored cum? If I asked him nicely, would he let me taste it?

No, no, no. I was a naughty girl for even thinking that.

Damn, but I wanted to be naughtier.

What happened in his office made me feel free, as if whatever restraints I'd put on my soul had given way with a big gush. I had no interest in strapping my emotions back down.

This weekend . . . If I had the guts, I was going to share the feelings in my heart. He might reject me, but he might tell me he felt the same.

I walked across the hall, back to my office with Raze right behind, joining me, Storm, and Luna.

Luna grinned, the look in her eyes suggesting she suspected me and Raze had been responsible for the banging.

I'd do it again once they left if he curled a claw my way.

"Let me grab some paper and a pen, and I'll take notes," I said.

"I'm so excited," Luna said, clutching Storm's hand.

He lifted their linked hands and kissed her fingers. "I can't wait to marry the woman of my dreams."

Aw. I sighed. This is one of the reasons I enjoyed this job. I spent much of my day surrounded by love.

"What do you have in mind?" Raze asked, sitting with his coat draped over his lap. Slick. I admired how quick he was.

"It sounds silly," Luna said. "But we'd like to be married at the pack meet-up spot. It actually has a great setup. There are cabins our guests can stay in, plus there's a bathroom and showers, and a kitchen. The caterer could come to us."

"Where the battle was held?" Raze asked.

"Yup." Luna nodded.

Battle? I'd ask later.

"All the packs will be there," Storm said. When they said packs, they referred to Storm's wolf shifter family and friends. Luna wasn't a wolf.

"What kind of meal would you like to serve?" I asked, jotting down notes.

They talked about their dream wedding, and I was thrilled I'd get the chance not only to be there to witness the wonderful event but to help them organize their special day.

Raze offered good insight, and despite us forming an

uneasy truce due to my pain-in-the-ass ex, we worked well together. Maybe, once Harris was run out of town, we'd make this permanent.

A girl could dream, right? I lived with others' dreams all day long. It was time one came true for me.

It was Raze. He was all I could imagine wanting for the rest of my days. I just had to convince him to make this the real deal.

We talked about other parts of their wedding, and they left.

After shutting my door, I sank back into my chair, facing Raze with my desk between us. Was now a good time to bring up the flavor of his cum?

He stared at his clasped hands on his lap, suggesting the imaginary steps we'd taken toward each other inside his office had been retracted.

"I'll see you tomorrow?" he said, standing.

Yeah, definitely stepping backward.

"Sure," I said lightly, despite the ache in my chest. "I have a ton of things to do at my apartment so I can take the weekend off." I didn't. "What time did you want to leave on Saturday morning?"

"About nine?"

I nodded. My heart was a solid lump in my chest, but what could I do?

I didn't like not knowing where we stood together, but I was anything but pushy.

Harris had pushed me, and I wouldn't do it to Raze.

If he wanted to step toward me again, I'd meet him more than halfway.

CHAPTER 16
RAZE

I'd backed away from Elisa, and I couldn't figure out why. I wanted to be with her more than anything, but a small voice in my mind told me I didn't deserve her. That I didn't deserve happiness and love. That I wasn't enough for her.

My damn father's words were intruding again.

I decided my mom was right—weren't they always?

I'd perform a cleansing tonight. Once ogre magic shoved him from my mind, I would be free to live the way I chose, not the way he'd tried to impose on me until the day he died.

"Are you okay?" Elisa asked as we locked up the office and walked to our vehicles. Due to size issues, monsters almost universally drove pickup trucks, though a few were known to buy used Hummers. We enjoyed having leg room and there wasn't anything worse than trying to stuff a big body into a vehicle made for a tiny human.

"I'm sorry I'm not talking much," I said. "I'm just thinking about this weekend."

"Stressing?"

"Definitely."

Her spine loosened. Being as honest as I could be was a good thing.

We stopped by her car, and I waited for her to get inside, scanning the area to make sure her ex wasn't lurking around.

"If you're having second thoughts about me going with you this weekend," she said, peering up at me forlornly from her seat. "I understand."

"Not one bit. I . . ." I fumbled to pull it from my pocket where it had been burning through my pants all day long. "I have something for you. It belonged to my mother."

"She runs Monstrous Munchies, right?"

"Yup, big sandwiches."

"I picked one up after work once and it took me two days to eat it," she said with a laugh, her posture loosening completely. I was glad I wasn't hurting her. "It tasted amazing."

"She loves to feed a crowd."

I gave Elisa the small silk bag.

"Your mother's, you said?" She stared down at it lying in her palm.

"Just something simple. I hope you like it." Mom had pulled it from her desk as if she'd had it there waiting since she set up the shop and handed it to me.

Elisa slid the simple gold chain from the bag and

carefully touched the red stone pendant dangling from it. "It's beautiful." She flashed me a smile, and I read so much affection in her gaze, it made my knees go weak. "I love the color."

Should I tell her it was a real ruby mined and exquisitely cut by Goreg's gargoyle clan?

"Would you help me put it on?" she asked, holding it out.

I bent forward and undid the clasp and laid it around her neck while she held up her hair. After securing it, I wanted to kiss her delicate nape.

But I needed to cleanse myself before I approached her again. If I messed this up with her, I'd never forgive myself.

"Thank you." She stroked the stone. "How many people do you expect this weekend?"

"If I know Mom, she's invited the entire town."

Elisa smiled. "That sounds be fun. What should I expect?"

"Ogre games."

"Like the Highland Games I went to once?" She explained what they were.

I nodded. "Something similar, though our games involve lots of mud."

"Mud and cum. Sounds like a fun crowd."

I loved how she could find humor in any situation. "I'd like to talk more about that this weekend." When we were alone. In a steaming pool. Hopefully naked.

"You want to talk about cum?" she quipped.

"If you'd like." Was that my voice coming out growly?

It sure was. My ogre heritage was shining through. Maybe it wouldn't be all that bad to throw her over my shoulder and bolt into the woods. Fulfill ogre tradition. How would Elisa take something like that?

"Let's find a moment this weekend to delve into it deeper." Now her voice was husky and, if I wasn't mistaken, full of need.

"I have to go," I said, my frenzy rising within me all over again. Until the cleansing ritual was finished, I wouldn't be free from my past.

Her heady smile fell. "Okay. I'll see you tomorrow, then." She shut her door and drove away.

I leapt into my truck and drove like a banshee let loose from the underworld to the apartment I rented in the back of the barn at Goreg and Violet's B&B.

Violet was working in the gardens out front, and she straightened, rubbing her back, waving as I drove past. Goreg made long sweeps across their big front lawn with a ride-on mower that was comically too small for his stony gargoyle frame. He spread his wings in greeting when he saw me before returning to watch where he was driving.

I'd have to wait until dark to perform the ceremony, but that gave me time to gather everything I'd need inside my apartment. It was a good thing I stuck to tradition like a good ogre and kept ingredients on hand—something my father would've nodded approval of rather than scold.

Inside my kitchen, I set a platinum tray on the counter, an item left over from when I lived a life so much different from this one. On it, I placed a vial of golden sand I'd collected on the edge of the Sirilean Sea deep within the elf realm. I was nearly out, and it was incredibly rare. I should have enough for this spell, and maybe another, though I'd cut it close. I didn't travel in that area often, so I didn't know when I could collect some more. Perhaps Tylik had some in his apothecary I could buy. He'd opened his shop a few weeks ago, and from what I could tell, he was doing well already.

I had to paw through my cupboard to find the next item, dragon's blood. When I originally collected it, I put it in a glass vial as it would melt through metal. It was a good thing ogres and dragons got along well. I couldn't imagine trying to obtain it if the dragon hadn't been willing to donate.

I added starlight powder in a stone container. We purchased it from sprites, one of the few species who could travel beyond the planet's outer atmosphere.

Crossing my kitchen to the fridge, I opened the door and grabbed the sealed package of moonflower petals, another item common in the elf realm. The pale pink, iridescent petals glowed and hummed within their container. The flowers lived, which wasn't unlike vegetation in the human realm other than these plants could uproot themselves and move, plus converse with anyone who cared to chat. They donated their petals. Forcing them would make them ineffective.

Before going outside, I removed all my clothing, carefully hanging each item up. I'd drop them at the dry cleaners tomorrow, along with the other suits I'd worn during the week.

Traditional rituals worked best if the person conducting it presented themself as close to their original form as possible.

I wrapped a towel around my waist and took the tray out to my small backyard, grateful Goreg and Violet had surrounded it with a fence. Dropping the tray onto my patio table, I squinted toward the little-used firepit for privacy. Wood had been stacked near the back of the fence. I suppose I should've carried it over while still dressed, but my father would've scowled to see me dirtying my clothing.

My growl erupted from my chest. "Good thing I'm doing the cleansing. Finally, Father, I'll put you—and your unwelcome advice—to rest forever." I wouldn't forget about him completely, though that would be a welcome side effect. His memory would be muted, like a distant dream.

I carried wood over to the pit and tindered it. Flames crackled in no time, and a nice, woodsy-smoky smell filled the air.

After bringing the tray over, lowering it to the grass near the fire, I sat, running the spell through my mind until it felt seamless.

The sun slipped below the horizon.

Once the world had gone fully dark, I purified the area around the fire. Then I drew a pattern in the dirt, a marking only an ogre would recognize. I placed a teal-colored candle in the middle of the symbol and lit it.

The sand sparkled and twitched as I poured it around the candle. I carefully placed the moonflower petals in the sand in an intricate pattern, making sure the tips touched. They hummed, their voices rising and falling in a lilting melody that sunk into my soul like the touch of a lover. It lulled me, and it was only when a log settled in the fire that I was brought back to the present.

"Don't do that," I chided the petals, though gently. This is why we kept moonflower petals in the refrigerator. Chilled, they remained silent. Warmed, they'd been known to put people into a trance. It could take a full coven of witches to break the spell, and witches were cranky. You'd have to give them your arm and firstborn—literally—to get them to perform a spell like that.

I took pinches of starlight powder and tossed it into the firepit flames, grinning as green and pink lights shot up like tiny fireworks.

Almost time.

Finally, I leaned over the candle and removed the stopper from the top of the dragon's blood vial, carefully releasing one drop onto the flame.

Scrambling backward, I rose to my feet and bowed, holding the position.

The flame roared, arching up from the candle, taking on the form of a dragon as big as me.

"What do you will?" the firedragon asked in a low, grinding voice.

"Greetings," I said, speaking the words I'd learned from . . . Yeah, I was trying not to think about him. When my father taught me basic spellcasting, I doubted he ever thought I'd use this one against him.

"Speak what you will," the dragon intoned. It was fading already. I could add more blood to renew it, but there should be enough time left in what I'd already used.

"My will unfolds," I said. "What I seek behold. I banish thoughts from far and low, never to think of my father again."

"As you wish, so it shall be." A blink, and the dragon fizzled, sinking back down into the candle.

The flame winked out, leaving me alone with the fire.

Who was I trying to forget with the cleansing spell?

My father. His memory felt too fresh in my mind, but perhaps the spell needed time to finish working.

"Hello?" someone called out from the walkway running beside the barn. Footsteps approached quickly.

Did I have time to run inside?

The gate I thought I'd locked creaked open, and Elisa stepped into my backyard.

"Oh, my," she said, her gaze drinking me in. "Raze?"

CHAPTER 17
ELISA

He slapped his hand over his cock but it was too late. The cat had been let out of the bag, so to speak.

I'd seen it. It was big and long and had small rings spiraling along the sides from the base to the tip.

"I apologize," he said, dipping forward in a bow. "I . . ."

I imagined he'd never had a woman walk in on him . . . I wasn't sure what he was doing. Barbecuing? He'd lit a fire in the pit, and a small teal candle burned beside it that could be for ambiance.

I wasn't sure why he was naked.

"You're naked because you're moon bathing," I suggested.

He shook his head, adding another hand to his groin. Still wasn't covering his delectable cock.

"Then you're naked because you're marking the area to keep wild animals away." I'd read about how male urine discouraged foxes and other creatures. Something about the hormones.

He shook his head again. His cock, meanwhile, was ready to party, thrusting up against his abs.

"I give up, then. I'm not sure why you're naked, but it's none of my business."

"I was performing a cleansing ritual."

I frowned. Cleansing . . . "Why? Were you dirty?"

His laugh snorted out. "Sometimes, I can be very dirty."

My grin rose. "I believe I'm dirty on occasion myself."

"Maybe we can get dirty together sometime."

Oh, hell, yeah. I took a step toward him. We could talk about his ritual later. For now, I wanted to—

"Why are you here?" he asked.

I cringed, my cheery mood fleeing. "I went to my apartment. I wanted to go inside, but Harris was standing on the front porch, waiting."

"You should've called me."

"I tried, but you didn't answer."

"Ah, yes. My cell phone is inside. I apologize again for not being available when you needed me."

Was he always this formal? Although, he'd just told me he sometimes enjoyed being dirty. I'd seen his squeaky-clean side. I wanted to roll around with him when he was feeling dirty.

"Allow me to dress, and we can discuss this." He grabbed a strip of cloth lying on the ground and wrapped it around his waist, sadly hiding his glorious cock. I felt proprietary about it; it was mine. Well, his, too, but mine as well. We were pretty much almost dating. That must come with some sort of benefits. "Shall we go inside?"

"I hate to disturb your ritual."

"I've finished, and I'm not sure it worked."

"Perhaps you need to do it again?" I pictured him dancing around the fire, completely naked. With a hard-on, of course. I'd stand in the shadows, watching, slowly stripping my clothing. I'd step out into the firelight, joining him. We could roll around and get dirty after that.

"I might," he said. As he passed me, he scooped up my hand and tugged me up the back stairs and into his kitchen, shutting the door behind me. He kept going, taking a short hall to a living room where he sat on the sofa, pulling me down to sit beside him. "Tell me everything."

"I parked but didn't get out of my car. I'm not sure he saw me." But I'd seen him sitting in the big wicker chair where I sometimes lazed on a Sunday morning, drinking coffee while surfing the web. "I kept the engine running, slouching down in the hope he'd get discouraged and leave. He knows my car. I don't know how he missed me."

"He's determined," Raze said with a growl.

"I know I should've gotten out of the car, strode up to him, and told him to leave, but I was scared." A shiver shot all the way out to my fingers and toes. "All I could think of was to come here."

"I'm glad you did." His arm went around me, and I snuggled into his side, sucking in his warmth. Spring had arrived in Monsterville weeks ago, bringing with it balmy weather. I had no reason to be cold.

"What can we do?" I asked, trying to ignore that he was pretty much naked.

Another growl ripped through him. "I believe I will have to kill him."

"No!" I lowered my voice. "No. You'll get in trouble."

He chuckled. "You're not disturbed about the thought of me committing murder?"

"I should be."

He grinned down at me. "I won't get in trouble. I'll make sure no one knows I did it."

"You're joking, right?" He had to be.

"I suppose. In the past, I could do it in public and get away with it."

I leaned away from him to study his face. "Ogres are allowed to kill each other?"

"Me, I said. I or anyone in my family could kill someone with our bare hands and the crowd watching would say nothing. Not a single protest would be voiced, not to our faces, that is."

"How is that possible?"

"I can't do that now, of course."

Nicely evasive. "Of course," I echoed.

"Since murder is out, we'll have to think of another solution. I have something in mind."

"What might that be?"

His level gaze met mine, and he bit down on his lower lip before releasing it. "I believe we should get engaged so you can move in with me right now."

CHAPTER 18
RAZE

I watched her face, hoping rejection wouldn't flash there.

"Do you mean it?" she asked in a breathy voice. "You want to take this from pretend dating to pretend being engaged?"

"Yes. Let's, um, pretend to be engaged and move you into my house. That'll keep him away, correct?"

"I'm not sure an engagement will make him leave town any more than you being my boyfriend, but it's worth a shot." She sighed. "I hate that I can't get him to leave me alone all by myself. Like, maybe I should be the one to kill him instead of you doing it. You got a knife around I could use?"

"I do, and I believe we could persuade Sheriff Venom that you have just cause for ending Harris's life."

"I can't do that, as you very well know."

I nodded.

"I love that you're stepping up to protect me," she said. "But do you understand what I'm saying?"

"It's never fun when you need someone bigger than yourself around to feel safe. You should be able to feel safe without me hovering at your side. But how is this any different from a woman hiring someone to be her bodyguard? That shows power and resourcefulness, not weakness."

"I guess I could hire a bodyguard."

I pressed my fist against my chest. "Consider it done."

"You're a sweet guy, Raze. Why were you so snarly all the time at Monica and Trevor's wedding?"

"Because I . . ." What would she say if I told her I'd acted that way because I was falling in love with her and was fighting it? I could see that now.

"Because why?" Her head tilted, and she watched my face.

She only wanted to pretend.

What could I do to convince her we should make this real? "I was a pain in the ass."

Her laugh snorted out, and I was glad I could make her grin when she was stressed. She nudged my side, and I savored her fingers on my bare skin. "You were okay."

"Just okay?"

"There were times . . ." Her eyes sparkled.

"Times?" I tugged her closer, savoring her leaning into my side.

My cock sensed possible action, poor thing, and perked up all over again.

"Times when I wanted to kiss you."

I turned her in my arms. "Elisa . . ."

She gazed up at me, her face open and happy. "What?"

"I think . . ." If I kissed her delicious lips, my frenzy would erupt. I'd take her to my bedroom and finish what we started. I'd bond myself to her and there would be no turning back. "I think I should get dressed, and we'll go get some of your things." I stepped out of her embrace.

"Alright." Her eyes shuttered, and I hated that I'd made that happen. Just like at the wedding, I was teasing her, then backing away. I did it to protect my heart, but at this rate, I'd drive her all the way across the country.

If she was living here with me, we'd be thrust together all the time. We'd sit in my backyard—me clothed, though perhaps not in a suit—and talk. Watch TV together. Eat at the same time and take walks down the road side-by-side, maybe even holding hands.

I could kiss her a few times. Maybe take things a little further.

That would make her fall in love with me, right?

CHAPTER 19
ELISA

I'd chewed through the tip of one fingernail and had started on the second when Raze pulled his big pickup truck into the driveway of my apartment building.

He put the vehicle into park and stared toward the porch taking up the front of the building. "I don't see him."

My breath whooshed out of me. "Maybe he left." Forever would be nice, but I doubted that was going to happen.

"I'll come in with you," he said, unbuckling.

We left the vehicle and took the walkway to the front of the building and climbed the stairs. My chair sat where I'd last left it. He hadn't move it or . . . I don't know, broken it.

I didn't know why I thought I'd find evidence Harris had been here. He was a jerk, but he was *not* a complete creep.

"Come on in," I said, unlocking my front door. The building housed three apartments, two small units on the first floor including mine, plus a larger three-bedroom that took up the entire second floor. Those tenants entered via a staircase on the right side of the building.

Inside, I peered around, still feeling nervous, though I couldn't figure out why.

"Woof." someone said from down the hall.

"Chickpea?" I called, eager to see my baby. I stooped down, expecting him to come scampering toward me like he always did, his little nails clicking on the hardwood floor. Even Raze wouldn't dissuade him. He loved meeting new people and would dance around their legs until they picked him up for cuddles.

Well, except for Harris, the only person my pup hated. He'd tried to bite my ex.

"Chickpea?"

He barked from ahead, and with fear hitching down my spine, I ran toward my tiny kitchen in the back, passing my living room and bedroom on the left. Other than a closet under the stairs and a bathroom attached to my bedroom, this was it. It wasn't much, but the rent was cheap.

I hit the kitchen at a dead run with Raze right behind me to find Chickpea trapped underneath my laundry basket. He peered through the slats and whimpered.

Dropping to my knees, I wrenched the basket away and snatched up Chickpea.

He licked my face, wiggling in excitement, his distress forgotten.

I scrambled to my feet and sagged into a chair at my kitchen table. I placed him on my lap, checking him all over, thankfully finding no wounds. His red bow lay on the floor, but other than that, he appeared unchanged. Except . . .

The bow had been sliced into pieces. A knife—used to cut the bow—lay on the counter, the tip pointing directly at where Chickpea had been trapped beneath the basket.

Message received.

"Harris did this," I hissed.

Raze's grim gaze swept the room, and I appreciated that he didn't question my assessment. I could point out that I kept my basket in my bathroom, not in my kitchen, but with Raze, I didn't have to. He believed me because I said it was so.

"I'm going to look around." He strode to the back door and made sure it was locked, tucking aside the sheer curtain to peer into the backyard. Before he left the kitchen, he stooped down in front of me.

Chickpea delicately sniffed his hand before licking it. He wiggled, straining toward Raze, a solid endorsement. Dogs were savvy. I should've ditched Harris when Chickpea snarled and tried to bite him.

"Are you okay?" Raze asked, his concerned gaze meeting mine.

I nodded. "I hope you don't mind my friend here moving in with you too."

"Your friend is more than welcome," he said in a rumbly voice. As if he knew instinctively how Chickpea loved to be patted, he scratched my pup's neck and rubbed his ears.

Drooling, Chickpea leaned into his touch, pretty much turning into a slug on my lap.

Eventually, Raze straightened. "Do you have rooms upstairs?"

I shared my apartment's layout.

"Wait here?" He strode toward the hall but paused in the opening, turning back. "Are you okay alone, or do you want to go sit in the truck?"

"I'm okay." I lifted my chin. Sure, I was scared, but if anything, anger dominated all my other emotions. How dare he? "Thank you."

With a nod, he strode into the hall.

I hugged chickpea, eventually putting him down when he squirmed. He trotted after Raze while I gathered his bed and toys. It didn't appear Harris had done anything else while he was inside my apartment.

Or so I thought until Raze strode back into the kitchen.

"I'll go grab some clothing," I said, dropping the bag with food on the table with Chickpea's crate, bed, and toys.

"We'll stop somewhere in town and pick up a few new things for you. We can get more tomorrow."

I frowned. "It won't take me long to pack."

Raze came over to me and held my arms, staring down at me solemnly. "Please don't go into your room."

CHAPTER 20
RAZE

My mother was right. Why did I ever doubt her?

The only solution to this was to kill Harris.

"What did he do?" Elisa asked, her voice rising to a shriek. "What did he do?" She wrenched away from me and ran to her room.

I followed and when she gasped while standing inside the doorway, I gathered her into my arms. "I'm sorry."

She peered up at me, shock lining her face. "Why did he destroy everything?" She eased away from me and walked among her shredded clothing lying on the floor. Her bedding had been yanked off the mattress, though I didn't look torn. "Why?"

Because he was possessive. Angry. And he wanted to cause her pain.

"He's a freakin' asshole," she shouted. "You hear that, Harris? You're an asshole!"

I doubted he'd remained here to hear her shriek, but

maybe he had. If someone hurt another, they often hung out to watch for a reaction.

At that thought, I bolted from the apartment and jogged around the outside of the building, finding nothing but a skunk who took one look at me and sashayed in the opposite direction with his tail spiked high.

When I didn't find evidence of Harris in the parking lot or on the street, I went back inside, finding Elisa sitting at the kitchen table again, holding Chickpea.

"Why does he always destroy things?" Tears streaked down her cheeks, and she swiped them away with the back of his hand. "Why won't he leave me alone? He didn't want me until I told him it was over."

It wasn't about wanting someone. Stalkers didn't like letting go of what they considered their possession.

"I have a plan for Harris," I said grimly. While killing him would give me a huge surge of satisfaction, there might be a simpler way to handle this.

She looked up, and I wanted to hold her and tell her everything would be alright. It would be soon. I'd save the words for then.

"What are we going to do?" she asked.

"It's time to cleanse you from Harris's mind."

ELISA

"Cleanse?" I said. "What does that mean?"

"It's a fairly simple process." His face scrunched. "When it works."

"I'm open to anything that'll keep him away from me forever."

"Exactly." He nodded as if he'd made up his mind. "First, we need to capture him."

I tilted my head. "Really?"

"Then I'll perform a cleansing ritual, only I'll direct the results at him."

"He's certainly dirty, but not in a good way like you, Raze."

A huge smile rose on his face. "That's very nice of you to say, Elisa."

"You're amazing."

"Even nicer." He leaned over and kissed my forehead. Chickpea leapt up and licked my chin.

I hugged my pup. "You said two things, though I'm

not sure I want to kidnap him."

"*Capture.* There's a big difference. Do you trust me?"

"I do." Deep in my heart, yes. My brain was arguing with my heart, however, suggesting that even scrubbing Harris with a wire brush wouldn't clean him up enough for my taste.

"We'll need to prepare everything at my apartment."

"Alright."

Not long later, I sat beside Raze as he drove us across town again. We'd stopped at a local department store where I'd picked up a few things while he waited with Chickpea in the truck.

Chickpea now rode on my lap, his front paws on the dash like he was a hood ornament, his nose twitching at everything we passed.

Harris's violation could've broken me, but I refused to give him that power. His actions were geared toward manipulating me, about making me suffer for pushing him away. I'd survived his attempt at ruining me once, and I'd do so again.

"When you caught me naked, I was performing an ogre ritual," Raze said.

"I thought you were moon bathing."

He snorted. "Maybe I should try that sometime. It might work just as well."

"What were you really doing?"

"A cleansing ritual, something from ogre tradition. If done correctly, the spell will drive a person from a some-one's mind."

"Who were you trying to forget?" I asked.

"My controlling, abusive father."

"Oh, Raze, I'm sorry." I scooted across the bench seat and leaned into his side, placing my fingers on his forearm as he steered the wheel. Chickpea came with me, looking affronted at first but then climbing across Raze's lap to look out the side window. "I didn't realize your relationship with him was that bad." I fingered the pendant he'd given me that I wore all the time, gliding it back and forth across the chain.

"He wasn't different from many other ogre fathers, and he had reasons to treat me in such a strict manner, but he's why I'm . . ."

"What?" I watched his face, but it remained neutral, as if he'd spent a lifetime learning to control every expression.

"It's why I wear suits all the time, and why I'm so . . . stiff." He winced.

"You're not that *stiff*. And I like how you fill out a suit."

He chuckled. "That almost makes me want to keep wearing them."

"I liked how you looked earlier too. When you wore only a towel and even better, when you didn't wear that."

"Sometimes, Elisa, you say the sweetest things."

"It's true."

"I don't know what to say." He turned the vehicle onto his road and drove to the end, parking in his drive and shutting it off.

Chickpea scrambled across me to look out my window.

Raze drew me up onto his lap. His tail coiled around my waist, and there was nothing more endearing than that. It made me feel protected and cared for.

I loved being held by him. This wasn't fake. *We* weren't fake. I didn't know where this was headed, but the path felt right.

"My father had many rules, and he strictly enforced them," he said. "It was for my own good."

"I assume you were a kid when he started this practice."

"Of course."

"Kids should be allowed to run around and have fun. Sit in the dirt, scoop it up, and toss it over their bodies." Not wear suits and behave stiffly.

"I was not allowed to do anything like that. I had to project the right image, that of my illustrious family, at all times." He stroked my back, and it felt good. I liked that we were talking, sharing things we wouldn't with others. We were adding planks on the new rope bridge stretching between us, making it more secure and safe.

"I don't know anything about ogre culture."

"That's probably not a bad thing."

"But it's you, and I want to know everything about you."

His arms tightened around me, and he kissed the top of my head.

I tilted my head to watch him. His voice was so solemn. Stiff, even, as if the training his father gave him had thickened his hide, and he didn't know how to peel it all away to reveal the real Raze beneath.

"I'm sorry about your dad, but your mother seems sweet," I said. "She always has a big grin on her face."

He gave me a true smile, one that warmed his eyes and made my heart flutter like a bird. "She loves making other people happy. Always has. It wasn't something my father appreciated."

"Did he impose rules on her too?"

"Always. As strict as the ones he set for me."

"I'm sorry. My home life might not have been the most wonderful, but I felt loved. My parents had very little, but what they did have, they shared with whoever had need."

"They sound wonderful."

I shrugged. "Times were tough, and they didn't always get along, but we had what we needed even if they wouldn't have agreed it was enough."

"I'm glad you had them." He stroked my cheeks. "My father was murdered."

I gasped. "Really? Did they catch whoever did it?"

He nodded slowly. "They were beheaded."

Whoa. "Do ogres have the same type of court system as humans?"

"Not really. They were caught in the act and taken to the courtyard immediately. They were strung up to wait until a crowd could gather the next day, and their heads were severed from their bodies to the audience's cheers."

"I can't . . . It sounds like something out of a movie set in another era."

"In many ways, that's ogres," he said. "We live life simply and with a system similar to your England of old. Kings, queens, a court, and many who have so much less than the royals." He sucked in a breath and released it. "We should get inside. I don't imagine Chickpea enjoys sitting in my truck."

Raze was sharing himself with me, and I hated to end our conversation, though it was making us both sad.

"You're right. I imagine he might like to go to the bathroom and have something to eat."

After Chickpea ran around on the lawn and did his doggie business, we took our things inside. There, my pup started sniffing, moving around each room. I imagined we'd see him again after he'd checked the entire place out.

I put down water and food for him. He'd find them when he needed them.

"Come upstairs, and I'll show you where you can sleep," Raze said.

I followed him up the stairs to a small landing. Violet and Goreg, who owned the B&B next door, had built this unit into the back of their big barn. It was cozy, comfortable. "I could go to a hotel."

"My fiancée?" Raze snorted. "Nonsense. You belong here with me."

He was right about that.

There was no place I'd rather be than with Raze.

CHAPTER 22

RAZE

"You can sleep here," I said, opening my bedroom door.

She strolled into the room. "I like it. Thanks." Her smile faded as she peered at the enormous bed again. "This is your room, right? Where are *you* sleeping?"

"Oh, I have a place."

She latched onto my arm before I could leave. "Where, Raze?"

"Well, see, I intend to get a guest bed for the other room, but I haven't been here long, and the room is still full of boxes." So many things I should've left behind when I left the traditional lands of my people. Instead, I'd clung to them as if possessions could make me complete.

I should've realized what I needed was already inside me.

She propped her hand on her hip. "What you're

saying is that you're going to squish your tall ogre frame onto that sofa downstairs, aren't you?"

"It's a comfortable sofa. I'll sleep well."

She stormed past me. "I'll sleep on the sofa. I'm not taking your bed."

"Want to share it then?" I called after her.

She froze in the doorway. "Is this a fake or real offer?"

I'd get down on my knees and beg if I thought it would make a difference. "I'm tired of pretending."

"I see." Her voice came out as stiff as my suits.

"I don't believe you do. I want this to be real, Elisa."

"What?"

"You heard me." I crept over to her and laid my big hands on her tiny shoulders. She was so much littler than me. If I tried to lie on top of her, I'd crush her. But fate kept thrusting us together for a reason, and I knew in my heart what it was. She was special; the only person I'd ever love. "I want this to be real. Will you be my true girlfriend?"

"Oh, Raze." Her voice broke.

Why wouldn't she turn and face me?

Oh, yes, I knew why. She didn't want to have to look me in the eye when she rejected me.

Suddenly finding it difficult to breathe through a tight throat, I released her shoulders and backed away. "I'm sorry. I guess I shouldn't have said that. We can go back to pretending." I wasn't sure my heart could take it, though I'd try.

She turned, and there were tears on her face.

I'd made her cry, and that ripped me apart almost as much as the thought she didn't want me.

"Yes, I want to be your real girlfriend," she said. "Really for real."

My pulse ground to a halt. "Really?"

She grinned. "Really."

I held out my arms, and she stepped into them.

CHAPTER 23

ELISA

His mouth seared across mine in a kiss so full of need it nearly broke my heart. But he'd already made my heart soar, and it wasn't coming back to the ground for days.

He turned and nudged me against the wall, keeping his mouth on mine. His tongue nudged my lips apart, and his tongue dove in, gliding across mine.

My skin burned wherever his fingers passed, first on my sides, then teasing across my belly. His palm slowly moved beneath my shirt and up over my breast, cupping me through my bra. His thumb claw stroked across my nipple, creating slow circles that drove my nipple to a hard bud. Warmth sunk through my bones. I wanted him, but I wasn't sure how to tell him.

A moan rose in my throat, and I lifted my hips up toward him.

He was so much larger than me. There was no way we could kiss and connect where I needed him most. But as long as he was with me and I with him, it would be enough.

His mouth left mine, and he traced the contours of my face with gentle kisses. Each felt like a sweet whisper of devotion. Pausing above me, he brushed our noses against each other.

With a slow smile, he said, "You're beautiful."

"So are you."

"I'm an ogre. You're a lovely human."

"You're a lovely ogre. I adore your horns." I tapped one. "Your tail." It coiled up along my side, and I stroked what I could reach. "And your coppery skin. But those are just the physical things I adore about you."

"You're making me blush, Elisa."

"I adore how kind you are to me, how you're patient. You might think you know it all when it comes to wedding planning, but you're willing to listen when I speak and change your mind if you see my idea's better than yours."

"You were doing well with my coppery skin and kindness," he said with a low laugh. "You should stop there."

I chuckled. "Maybe we shouldn't talk. We have other things we can do, don't we?"

"How far do you want to take this?"

"As far as it feels right."

"Then let's see if we can make this feel so much better than right."

He kissed me, making my heart ache and my pulse roar through me. His fingers made quick work of my clothing, as mine did with his, and our laughter bubbled inside us as we scrambled out of our things while still kissing. I liked that I could laugh with him, that even in this, we could have fun.

When I was naked other than the pendant he'd given me, he backed me against the wall again. I leapt and wrapped my legs around him. He was so much taller than me, but he somehow scrunched forward enough to keep kissing me.

The end of his tail glided around my waist, tugging me closer while supporting me so his hands could remain free.

He stroked my arms and along my sides, slowly teasing closer to my breasts, and I savored the feel of being this close to him.

His big cock rose between us, and I couldn't wait to feel it inside me.

The tip of his tail glided through my wet folds and slid across my clit.

I pumped against him, whimpering, determined to hold on until we'd both finished. I could tell I was going to come like never before.

He stroked beneath my breasts, moving slowly toward my nipples. His claws caressed them before he rolled them with his rough fingertips.

I arched my spine, crying out at how wonderful this felt.

His tail was firm yet gentle as it teased me close to the edge of the abyss, rolling across my clit before the head dipped inside me.

I shivered from his touch, my every nerve ending on fire.

Keening, I pumped against him. My heart raced, but it was filled with so much tenderness for him. I wanted to make this as special for him as he was making it for me.

My nipples pebbled, and he cupped each one in turn, flicking them with his claws while his tail continued its slow dance against my clit before teasing inside me.

I bucked against him, thrusting toward each slow, languid stroke.

"I need . . ." I whimpered.

"This?" he asked, pushing the thick head of his tail inside me. "Or this?" He pulled it out and replaced it with the tip of his cock, pushing only a fraction of it into my folds.

"Both."

"I don't believe you can handle both, Elisa," he said gravely, watching my face.

"Try."

"I'm big."

"Very."

He chuckled low and deep, and I could tell I'd pleased him. "Let's start with just my cock. We can try other things later."

Now that his tail was no longer inside me, focused on my clit, rubbing and stroking while he rocked his hips against me. Each push forward drove his cock a little deeper. He was thicker at the base. Would I be able to take all of him?

He slowly shifted forward before dragging his hips back. The stretch of each thrust was exquisite, a mix of pain and pleasure, and I wouldn't have it any other way.

Panting, I clung to his shoulders, spreading my legs wider to accommodate his girth.

"I want you," he said, curling forward to kiss my forehead.

"Take me. I need you."

"Yes." With a forward drive and a heady growl, he seated himself inside me. He paused, watching my face. Did he think he was hurting me? Yeah, he was big, but he felt amazing.

"Are you going to watch me, or are you going to give me the best orgasm of my life?" I asked him with a low laugh.

"I'm going to give you many best orgasms of your life, each one an improvement over the last."

"No talk. Action." I shook my finger between us, but I was only teasing.

"You want action?" he asked with a grin. "Watch what an ogre can do."

RAZE

I moved within her, making each stroke slow and tender to give her body a chance to adjust to mine. It hadn't been easy getting my cock inside, though her eager wetness helped.

She clung to me, breathing fast, her tiny whimpers of joy echoing around us.

"I can't believe we're finally together, doing something I've only dreamed of since I first met you," I whispered.

"You wanted to fuck me the moment you met me?"

"You irritated me so much. I wanted to show you what happened to wiseasses."

"Are you showing me now?" she said pertly, with a sly gleam in her eyes. "Because this feels too tame for something like that."

My jaw dropped. "I'm trying to be gentle."

"Maybe I don't want gentle? I mean, I don't want you to drive me through the wall, though the idea has merit.

But I want you to let go. Show me the Raze who's been locked down all his life. Show me wild. Show me *you*."

The frenzy churning inside me locked onto that idea, urging me on.

"You amaze me all the time, Elisa."

"Show me," she said with a wink. "Take off that suit, toss it aside, and show me the true Raze."

"I don't want to hurt you."

"I'll tell you if something gives me pain."

"Alright." I started moving faster, still taking care, but emboldened by her cries of pleasure. It was all I could do not to unleash my frenzy.

"Yes, like that. You're getting better at this, Raze!"

Better, huh? I'd show her better.

I loved that she could tell me what she needed, that she didn't worry about feeling embarrassment or what I might think. It made me go feral, something that had never happened in my life.

Moving faster, I twisted my hips, driving my cock deeper.

"Good. Feels good," she said, her forehead pressed against my chest. "More."

"I saw this one in a movie once." Shifting her hips higher, I spread her wide and squatted as I pulled out, rising to hit her clit before sliding inside.

"Yes. Wild. Do it, Raze."

I wanted to be the male she needed, but even more, I wanted to be me, a male come undone by the feelings he had for his mate. She wanted untamed, something I'd never offered, and I wanted to give it to her.

Something snapped inside me, and I went faster, driving hard as she cried out in joy.

My foot caught on something, and I shifted sideways, trying to adjust my position. I lost my balance.

Latching onto Elisa, I tumbled sideways, crashing onto the floor with her in my arms, lying across my chest. Miraculously, we remained connected, though I'd lost my rhythm.

She lifted her head. "Somehow, the movies always make wall sex look easy, don't they? This stuff is hard."

"I'm hard," I shifted my cock up to embed it deeply within her. The cold floor felt amazing under my back.

She sat up and started riding me, rising and slamming herself down. Her breasts jiggled, and her hair was a wild disarray. I'd never seen anyone prettier in my life.

Caught up in the moment, I drove my cock up to meet each of her downward thrusts. We moved together so well, a dance of lust and the beginning of love.

She would remain in my heart through this lifetime and beyond.

CHAPTER 25
ELISA

I could ride him like this for the rest of my life. Heat spiraled inside me as I lifted and let my body's weight drive me back down. It was amazing, but damn, what a workout. How did guys do it? All that pistoning of their hips while bracing themselves over whoever they loved.

He must've sensed my thighs were burning. Or I was slowing, which was pretty sad when I was this heated. He sat and twisted around so I was beneath him, then pulled himself out.

"No," I whimpered, clinging. "Need more thrusting."

He chuckled. "I promise more thrusting. I'll thrust into you tonight and all day tomorrow if you want."

"Yes. All the time."

He rolled me over onto my belly and lifted my hips. Placing the head of his cock at my opening, he held me steady while jerking forward, embedding himself once more. "Like this?"

My eyes rolled back in my head. "Oh, yeah."

"We're in a movie, Elisa. Just watch us."

"At least there's not far to fall," I said, grinning. How could I be so into this yet still find humor in the situation? Probably because this was real and gritty and us. Not something made up or fake.

Just Elisa and Raze grinding together.

He started moving faster, holding my hips in place, and sensations swirled through me. My bones went weak, and my pulse shot through the top of my head.

I moaned and gasped as he increased the tempo. The pleasure that rushed through my body was unbeatable. I was completely exposed, completely vulnerable, and completely in love with everything he did to me. He moved within me, and I responded in kind, driving my hips towards his, meeting him thrust for thrust.

The heat of the moment was almost too much to bear, and I could feel my climax building with each passing second. My entire body was melting, merging with his.

Deep, powerful sensations grew within me, generated by Raze. They radiated from my core and outward. Every inch of me was alive with prickles, and my body quivered with delight.

With a groan, he alternated his strokes to glide across every inch of my inner walls.

My muscles contracted and relaxed in perfect harmony, and my skin was ultra-sensitive to the touch.

A powerful feeling of euphoria rushed through my body, filling it with emotions I'd never experienced before. They were fully wrapped up in Raze, my wild, sweet ogre.

My muscles tensed and relaxed as I rocketed toward complete satisfaction.

I panted, my breathing ragged, and with each of his thrusts, I moaned. His groans joined in as his body tensed and his cock grew stiffer.

His fingers tightened on my hips. I was so close. Yes, right there.

When his tail coiled around my waist and stroked my clit, that was all it took. My orgasm jolted through me, starting in my core and zipping out to my fingers and toes. It shook me, took me.

And there was no one I'd rather experience it with than Raze.

CHAPTER 26
RAZE

After breakfast and washing up, because . . . Yes, I did have a lot of cum, I sought Goreg at the B&B.

"I'll definitely help," he'd said. "And I'll track down my brothers."

A bunch of our friends came over, meeting up with us in the small backyard behind my barn apartment. We ate a late lunch, and I introduced my plan.

"Could you explain this further?" Goreg asked. He sat in a lawn chair beside his wife, Violet.

Storm and Luna played frisbee nearby, but they were listening.

Elisa sat on my lap with my arms and tail around her. After holding her in my arms all night, I didn't want to release her. We'd joked about it this morning, taking a shower together and even bumping sides as we cooked breakfast in my kitchen.

While everyone listened raptly, Elisa and I had explained about Harris.

"I was thinking about casting an ogre spell," I said.

"Ogres do spells?" Max asked. He and his wife, Chastity, sat to the right of Goreg.

I dipped my head forward. "They're not much. Some moondust and a drop or two of dragon blood."

"Dragon blood?" Luna shouted. She slapped her hand over her mouth. "Sorry. Neighbors. I forget everyone's not as into monsters as me." Striding over to Storm, she hugged him. "Love my monster."

"Wolf, sweetie. *Wolf*," he said with a fanged grin.

"What kind of spell are we talking about?" Chastity asked. She pushed her glasses up the bridge of her nose. Her and Max's daughter, Sydnee, sat on her lap, facing us. She cooed and kicked her tiny feet, waving her arms in the air.

"It's a forgetting spell I tried the other night with mixed results," I said. Maybe it worked a little? I no longer felt like I must wear a suit. Look at me, wearing shorts and a t-shirt! But the rules my father had beaten into my bones still lingered, snarling and snapping at me to obey. Whatever "progress" I'd made came solely from spending time with Elisa. She brought out the real me, and I clung to it, not wanting to let go. "I'm not sure the spell did much. And I'm almost out of dragon's blood, so I'll need to get some from Tylik. I'm not sure I have enough for the spell."

"Not even asking how you guys get dragon blood," Elisa said. "I doubt there's a blood donation center nearby."

There could be.

"Maybe you didn't have all the right ingredients?" Max said, his arm loosely around Chastity's shoulders. He teased her hair, gliding his fingers through it. "My mom might be able to help. She's friendly with some witches. She could ship some to you."

"Witches?" Chastity asked. Sydnee squealed, following it up with a giggle. Poor Chickpea must be used to only one person being around. He kept jumping at the squeals and yipping, racing around us before putting his front paws on Chastity's leg.

"Witches are rare." Max nodded as if agreeing with himself. "And ornery. I doubt they'd be willing to cast a spell on a human. They, like us, are just trying to fit in."

A valid point.

"We can't wait for your mom to ship us ingredients," I said. "Harris is a pain in the ass. I'm trying to avoid killing him. He threatened Chickpea. *Elisa*." My voice came out with a growl.

"Sitting here," she said, though humor filled her voice. "I'm okay. Harris won't hurt me. I think."

I think wasn't good enough for me.

At hearing his name, Chickpea yipped and scampered over to leap on my right thigh, leaving Sydnee sobbing and straining to reach the dog.

"Nap time," Max said, rising. "I left the bassinet in your kitchen. Can I lay her down in your room?" he asked me.

"Of course." I scooped up Chickpea and dropped him on Elisa's lap.

While Chickpea tried to lick my face, Max lifted

Sydnee into his arms. Rather than cooing like she usually did when she saw her dad, she kept sniffling, burying her face in his neck, smearing her tears on his shirt.

"Let's get you inside, little love," he said, patting her back.

Chastity rose. "She might need to nurse."

Max carried her into my apartment with Chastity walking beside them.

"If we're talking spells," Goreg said. "You might want to clear anything you do with the local coven."

No, thanks.

Violet sat close to Goreg, his left wing around her back and her hand resting on his thigh. I loved seeing them so in tune with each other. While I hadn't helped with their wedding plans at all, that didn't matter. They were friends, and they were blissfully happy together.

"There are truly witches?" Elisa asked, looking up at me. "Why am I asking?" Her low laugh rang out, a seductive sound that made my cock twitch. I really shouldn't get turned on by her closeness when we were hanging out with friends. "Of course witches exist. I'm sitting in our backyard chatting with an orc, a gargoyle, and a wolf shifter. And you, my delightful ogre."

I scrunched over to kiss her neck.

She'd said *our backyard*. I loved that she saw us together, that this was our home now, not just mine. No more sitting by the firepit alone. No more watching romcoms without someone beside me to laugh at the fun parts. No more sleeping by myself.

Luna tossed the frisbee to Storm, who shifted into his

wolf form, leaping into the air and catching it in his teeth, much to Luna's amusement.

Her laughter rang out. "I'm listening. I promise."

Storm shifted back seamlessly and threw the frisbee to Luna. "I like the witch idea, but I wouldn't want to tackle the local coven."

"Nobody would," I said. "We'll use the ingredients I already have, and we'll avoid witches. What are your thoughts about doing it tonight?"

"So soon?" Luna asked. "Can you be ready? You said you're almost out of dragon blood."

"Sure," I said. "All I need to do is grab Harris, bring him here—bound of course—and perform the spell."

"How are you going to grab him?" Elisa asked with a frown. A butterfly flitted around my small backyard and landed on her outstretched hand. Like a fairytale princess—or queen, I supposed—she could lure anyone to her touch.

My heart swelled with love for her, so big, it might explode. What a way to go.

The butterfly took off, and the rest of us exhaled. Even Chickpea had remained motionless when the butterfly landed.

"What?" Elisa said, looking around with a look of pure joy on her face. "Why did we stop talking about a plan?"

Chickpea leapt up to lick her chin.

"We . . . took a break, love," I said, sitting forward to kiss her cheek. "We can get back to it now. You know you're special."

"So are you," she said, poking my chest gently. Her voice lowered. "So very special, Raze." She nuzzled my neck, whispering. "When can we disappear together?"

Soon, I hoped.

"Back to the plan," Goreg said, though his fingertips teased across Violet's belly where her top had ridden up, and Storm and Luna kept kissing. "We capture him and bring him back here."

"Not until dark. The spell works best then," I said. *If* it worked. I still wasn't convinced, but what else could we do?

"How do you propose grabbing him?" Violet asked. "We've got a decent rapport with our demon sheriff, but I don't believe he'll take kindly to us kidnapping a human."

"Harris won't go easily," Elisa said. "He'll scream and fight, though I know you guys could subdue him fairly quickly."

"Who needs kidnapping?" someone called out from my open kitchen door. Darrow strolled down the short flight of steps, holding hands with his girlfriend, Paige.

They'd recently bought a house with a big backyard where they planned to showcase his statues. Not the one on the lawn. That one was special.

"Me, Max, and Storm planned to *persuade* someone to come back here with us tonight," I said. "No kidnapping." It was all about perspective.

"Is this the fun kind of persuasion or another kind?" Darrow asked, looking between us.

Paige chuckled. "I'm in no matter what kind it is."

"My thought was to leave you women here," I added.

"Hell, no," Elisa said. "If we're going to kidnap Harris, my stalker ex who won't leave me alone," she added for Darrow and Paige's benefit, "then I'm coming with you. You don't know where to find him."

"*We* do," Goreg said. "My brother, Murtik, is on a reconnaissance mission right now. I took the liberty of enlisting his help earlier. He'll report in—" He squinted up at the sky. "There he is now."

Murtik swooped in, circling over us before landing lightly on the clipped lawn. He strode over, his glance landing on each of us.

When I first met Goreg's brother, he'd come across as superficial. Even stuck on himself. According to local rumors, he was one of the hottest gargoyles in town. A playboy gargoyle, if there was such a thing.

But then I'd gotten to know him. He wrote poetry, and it was good. Everyone hired him to do their interior design. And he loved working with precious stones, something gargoyles were known for. They not only mined the stones, but they also crafted them into exquisite works of art and sold them. Murtik was considered one of the best. A male could get a complex around someone like that.

Violet rose and barreled into Murtik. "Where've you been, brother-in-law?"

He hugged her and tenderly kissed her cheek. "I've been around."

"You haven't stopped by for Uncle Bub's scones in

forever," she said with a pout. "My uncle's getting mighty pissed."

Murtik chuckled. "Then tell him I'll be by this Saturday and to hold back three scones for me."

"I will." She skipped back to Goreg and settled on his lap with his wings wrapped around her.

"What did you find out?" Goreg asked his brother.

"Harris entered his office ten minutes ago," Murtik said. "I believe that'll be the best place to . . . apprehend him."

"Kidnap," Storm said. "We're grabbing him, tying him up, gagging him—"

"Yay," Luna shouted.

He grinned. "And bringing him here for the spell."

Murtik looked toward Goreg. "If you're all set, I need to get going." He flashed his fangs our way. "I have a date."

Goreg rolled his eyes. "Thanks for your help."

"Any time." Murtik took flight and soared from view.

"This all sounds lovely, but as for kidnapping, I think we *women*," Violet rolled her eyes, "Jeez, you guys. Getting back to that. Do you really think we're just help-less human females unable to protect ourselves?"

"I do appreciate my wolf's protection," Luna said, tossing the frisbee toward Storm.

He shifted fast and caught it in his fangs before returning to his human shape to throw it back to her. "I come in handy every now and then."

"That you do, honey," she said.

"I'm not saying you can't defend yourself," I said.

Elisa shook her head, though her sparkling eyes told me she wasn't mad. "Sure, you are."

"We can't *all* go after Harris," I added. "There are lots of other things that need to be done if you want to be helpful."

"Thank you," Elisa said. She put Chickpea down, and he raced over to Storm and Luna to zip back and forth between them, chasing the frisbee.

I tightened my arms around Elisa. "I worry Harris will see us coming and hide."

"I wouldn't put it past him," she said. "But if an ogre, an orc, two gargoyles, and a wolf come after him, he'll bolt. Let alone human women."

"That could be the best way to handle it," Luna said. "If all of us go after him, he'll take off, and you'll never see him again."

"The idea's wonderful, but you don't know Harris," Elisa said. "He might hide, but he'll be back. He doesn't give up easily. If he did, me telling him we were through and leaving town would be enough. Instead, he followed me here. Then he threatened Chickpea to make me cooperate. He'll keep after me until he makes me say I want to be with him," she grumbled. "Which is not happening. If I did, though, he'll promptly go back to his irritating self until I left him again."

"I'd be happy to help you guys grab Harris," Darrow said. He and Paige had settled on my back steps in the shade.

Paige nodded. "Darrow's perfect for the job."

Ah, yes. That was right.

My gorgon friend could handle this all by himself if needed.

But would he?

CHAPTER 27

ELISA

"What can Darrow do?" I asked.

"No." Darrow's voice came out kind but final. His thick, gray bands of hair spiraled around his head before settling along his shoulders and back. Did they reflect his mood? I sensed so. A starkness filled his gorgeous teal eyes. "I do it when it's needed, but I'll never indiscriminately turn someone to stone." A small shudder went through him, and Paige put her arm around the back of his waist. The look she sent us suggested if we didn't let this go, we'd have to challenge her to get to the guy she loved.

Even without her protective presence, the steel in his gaze and the paleness of his light gray face told me this was a tender subject.

"Do what?" I asked.

"He's a gorgon," Raze said.

"Oh, turn him to stone," I said.

Darrow's soft gaze met mine. "Here's the thing. I've

been dealing with one stone guy longer than I'd like, so I've promised myself I'm not changing anyone unless absolutely necessary. I'm quite open to a temporary freeze, however, if it's needed, but can we try to avoid it?"

I imagined people would be eager to take advantage of his gorgon abilities. Many had probably tried.

"I'll go with you," Darrow said. "I want to help. We'll see what we're dealing with there and do what we need to do after that. If I'm there, and firmer action is needed, I'll do it, but only then."

I wasn't worried too much about Harris hurting my friends. They were monsters, for heaven's sake. One and a half times his size. Raze could crush him with one hand. And Harris had never been one for weapons, though there was always a first time. If he was desperate enough, who knew how he'd behave?

"We'll all go together, then?" I said.

"He'll see us coming," Storm pointed out, joining us, holding Luna's hand. The frisbee lay on the lawn, waiting for the next round. Chickpea leapt around it, barking.

"We might be able to sneak up on him more easily if it's just a few of us," Luna said.

I lifted my chin. "I want to be a part of this. Do you think he won't notice monsters creeping up on him?"

"What do you suggest?" Paige asked. "I think we should participate, but he's stalking you. If anyone should grab him, it should be you."

"There's more to taking care of this problem than

just capturing him," Raze pointed out. "Once we get him back here, we need to keep him from escaping or alerting the neighbors."

"Yeah, they frown on us enough already," Violet said. "Gargoyles!" She faked a shiver. "But honestly, most are super nice. They can see past scales, fur, and horns to the person inside, and I appreciate that."

"I believe two or three of us should retrieve Harris," Darrow said, his thoughtful gaze directed to the ground. "While the others gather whatever you'll need for the spell."

"Raze and I are the only ones who know what Harris looks like," I said.

Luna sheepishly raised her hand. "Me and Storm do."

Ah. I wasn't going to chide them for getting other quotes for their wedding. I operated a business, and I kept that separate from friendship.

"It's not what you're thinking," she said. "We ran into him at Rylee's cupcake shop, and he introduced himself to us after he heard me sharing our wedding plans with Rylee."

I squirmed. "I didn't *exactly* think you went to the competition."

"Well, if you did, that's okay, too," Luna said simply. She grinned. "If it helps any, me and Storm have already decided to hire you and Raze to manage our wedding."

Good news among the unsettled feelings. "Thank you."

"What do you need for the spell?" Darrow asked.

"Golden sand collected from the edge of the Sirilean Sea," Raze said.

"Elf realm stuff," Max said, joining us. "Chastity's still nursing Sydnee but will be down soon. What did I miss?"

"We're choosing who's best for each task," Raze said. "We haven't decided who'll go after Harris, but we were talking about splitting up. Some could obtain the necessary ingredients. Others will need to purify the area around the firepit. I did it last night, but it needs a redo."

"What else do you need?" Storm asked.

"As I said, I'm almost out of dragon blood."

"I think it's so cool that there are dragons," Luna breathed. "I picture them delicately holding out a hand—"

"Paw, sweetie," Storm said. "They'd be horrified to hear you calling their mitts a hand."

"Whatever." She rolled her eyes but grinned. "They hold out their paws and a clinical person will carefully prick the tip. Blood will drip, and they'll collect it in pretty vials."

"You've got an incredible imagination," I said. I turned to Raze. "Is that how it's done?"

"Sort of," he said, scratching the back of his neck. I suspected there was much more to it than Luna's fantasy, but it was clear we might never hear all the details. "I've got plenty of starlight powder and moon-flower petals," he said.

"Wonderful." I shook my head at the idea of starlight powder and moonflower petals. I might be comfortable with monsters, but there was still so much to their world I'd yet to discover.

"Where can we get the ingredients?" Luna asked. "I'm picturing a shop with eye of newt and all kinds of creepy things lining the shelves."

"You might be disappointed," Max said. "The apothecary's not that exciting."

"I think you're right," I said with a sigh. "We'll have to split up. There's so much to do. Max, do you know where we can get supplies locally?"

He nodded, his gaze meeting Raze's. "Tylik."

I continued. "Raze, you, Darrow, and Paige can go after Harris. Three should be enough, right?"

Raze grunted agreement.

"Darrow, I bet you and Raze can immobilize him and keep him from calling the police," I said. "Paige can supervise and drive the getaway car."

"I want to gag him," Paige breathed. She was getting into this too much, but enthusiasm was welcome.

"I assume Chastity will need to stay here with the baby," I said. "That leaves me and Max going to the shop for supplies. Storm, do you know how to purify the area? You, Luna, Goreg, and Violet could do that."

"Before we leave," Raze said, "I'll show you where the supplies are and what needs to be done.

"I'll go tell Chastity where we're going," Max said, heading into the apartment.

"We won't let him get away," Paige said. "We'll nab him and have him back here in no time."

I hoped so. Too much could go wrong with this plan.

We might grab Harris, obtain the ingredients, purify the area, and then the spell might not work.

"Will the spell work on humans?" I asked.

Max paused outside the kitchen, and a smile teased across his lips. "It's been done many times."

Oh, my.

What had monsters made us forget before they decided to join us?

CHAPTER 28

RAZE

We piled into Paige's sedan, me squishing into the back.

"I could ride back there," Paige said as she climbed into the driver's seat. "There's no reason for you to take the second row."

"It's your car. You should drive." I had to hunch forward, pretty much burying my chest in my lap to keep from poking my head through the Jeep's soft top roof. And my legs had to splay wide.

"We should've switched vehicles with Max." Max had taken my truck, deciding to leave his vehicle with Chastity in case she needed it. Goreg and Violet's vehicle was at the shop, and Storm had taken the back seat out of his Jeep the week before and hadn't put it back in.

"I really don't mind," Paige said.

Darrow settled in the passenger seat. His hair swirled around his head. Was he nervous about this? I was. Hard not to be. So many things could go wrong.

"We're not going far," I said. "Just to the mall. His business has an entrance on the outside wall." There was no way I'd let Paige ride back here. She was a special female, Darrow's mate. I was . . . well, a friend. One who could ride in the back seat.

Darrow tugged his seat forward, and that helped.

"Should we wear trench coats?" Paige asked as she started her car and backed down the drive. "Hats? Maybe masks."

"Why?" I asked.

"A disguise," she said with a roll of her eyes in the rearview mirror

"Darrow and I have rather distinctive appearances, though I'm not wearing a suit." The back of my neck itched, and my heart kept telling me to go back to my apartment and put on a suit. I only wore a t-shirt and shorts. So incredibly informal. What if someone . . . I halted the thought. It didn't matter if anyone saw me other than when I was hauling a screaming Harris from his shop. I'd rather no one saw that.

I held up my hand as Paige started taking her vehicle down the road. "Hold on."

She came to a screeching stop. A centaur trotting along the sidewalk beside two tiny centaurs gave us a glare before taking their hands and picking up her pace.

"Sorry," I whispered, though she wouldn't hear.

"What's the problem?" Darrow asked, turning to look back at me.

"Do you have anything in your trunk?" I asked Paige.

"Nope, empty. Perfect for our devious plan." She was

enjoying this too much. "He'll fit." A grin rose on her face before her lips smoothed. "Shall we continue?"

At my nod, she took the vehicle to the stop sign and turned right, continuing across town to the mall, where she parked in the lot outside Love & Lace.

"Looks like someone's inside with him," Darrow said, staring in that direction.

"We'll wait until it's near closing time," I said, leaning back in the seat. "The spell can't be performed until dark, so we have plenty of time."

The clock ticked slowly. The couple Harris was speaking with left, but another arrived before we could get out of the car. I was beginning to think we might need to grab him in the lot when he left for the day, though I'd prefer to do it inside where no one would see. I wasn't worried about humans interfering. Who'd tussle with a monster?

Our demon sheriff appeared to be on our side, but kidnapping someone was a little different from defending Elisa in a restaurant. Venom would only keep his job if he made sure everyone obeyed the rules.

Finally, the second couple left.

"Now?" Paige asked, her fingers beating a steady rhythm on the steering wheel. "It's almost six. He must be closing soon, and it's starting to get dark."

"He's putting things away," Darrow said, opening his door. "It's time."

We got out and raced to the wall of the mall, skirting close to the surface to avoid detection. Actually, Paige did that. I shook my head and strode along like usual, still feeling awkward wearing such informal clothing.

Darrow's hair swirled like a tornado around his head, showing he was as nervous about this as me.

We reached the glass front of Love & Lace and paused.

"Who first?" Paige asked. With another grin, she held up her finger. "I know! Darrow and I will go inside and distract him." She leaned into his side. "We can pretend we need to talk about our wedding plans, sweetie. We'll make sure Harris turns away from the front door. He won't suspect a thing. Raze, you can peek inside and wait for the right chance to pounce."

Pounce? Sigh.

"An excellent plan," Darrow said, kissing her forehead. At least his hair had calmed down. "Back the car over, closer to the store. No need to attract too much attention when we haul him out."

With stores closing, the parking lot was nearly empty.

Paige tossed me the keys.

"I assume you brought rope," Darrow said.

"Got it." I held up a paper bag with a bunch of bandanas we could use to bind him and as a gag. Contrary to what he might think, I'd never done anything like this. Ogres had a rep for stomping around and harming others, but we were actually quite civilized. The height of sophistication as far as beasts go, according to the magazine, *Uptown Monster*.

"Alright, then," Darrow said. "Give us a few minutes."

They held hands as they walked into the shop. Seeing them, Harris called out a greeting.

I waited, carefully peering through the glass. Sitting at his desk facing this way, Harris had his planner open. Since it was getting late, it appeared he was trying to set up a future appointment for Darrow and Paige.

Paige kept trying to lure him over to some photos mounted on the back wall. There, his back would face the front of the shop.

Finally, he joined her, and Darrow followed, his hair floating around his head.

I dropped the paper bag and removed the bandanas, tucking them into the back pocket of my shorts.

When Paige had engaged Harris at the posters on the wall, I rushed across the front of the shop and carefully eased open the door. As quietly as I could, I advanced toward Harris. I'd grab his hands and bind them while Darrow wrapped a gag around his head. After that, it shouldn't be too hard to tie his ankles. We'd toss him in the trunk and race back to my apartment.

But when I was a few feet away, Harris whirled around. His leg shot out in a solid martial arts kick, hitting me hard in the gut. As an ogre, I naturally had granite abs, so his kick didn't do more than jar me. Neither did his upper cut to my jaw. I did grunt. I hadn't sparred with anyone in ages. When my mother and I split from the rest of the ogres, we told ourselves we were leaving everything related to our background behind.

I'd let myself grow soft.

When Harris released a screech worthy of the star of a karate movie and a tornado kick, I dove to the right, rolling and coming up to a crouch.

"You liar," Harris fumed, rushing toward Paige.

Darrow might be on a hiatus, but no one and nothing was going to harm the love of his life.

He released his gaze, and teal light shot from his eyes, hitting Harris. He froze with his arms clawing toward Paige and his face full of fury.

"Well," Paige huffed, sagging against the wall. She recovered quickly and ran around Harris, leaping into Darrow's arms. They kissed, and a growl rumbled in his chest. When they pulled apart, she held his shoulders, staring into his eyes.

"Love," she whispered. "I'm sorry."

"It's not your fault."

"*I'm* sorry," I said.

"Not your fault, either, though thanks," Darrow said with a nod in my direction.

Paige slid down his body to her feet and they separated, though they maintained contact with linked hands.

"Okay," I said, rubbing my palms together. "I take it we won't be tying him up and gagging him."

"He won't be moving or screaming," Darrow said grimly. "Let's get him outside."

Fortunately, only a few vehicles passed in the lot as I carried Harris out to Paige's car over my shoulder. She popped open the trunk and waved to the interior.

I stuffed him headfirst inside, but his legs stuck out the back.

"Anyone got orange tape?" I asked. "We can tie it to his foot."

"The bandanas," Paige said, racing back to the shop. But the door had locked behind us. "Shit. No bandanas." She returned to her car.

We stared at Harris's lower body sticking out from the back of her trunk. Unfreezing him wasn't an option; he'd run.

"Ideas?" Darrow asked.

Paige frowned before her gaze slid to the vehicle's roof racks.

CHAPTER 29

ELISA

We entered Mystic Mixtures, a shop I'd missed despite its location in the middle of town. In fact, I would've strode right past it if Max hadn't grabbed my arm and tugged me inside. Was it magically protected from human interest?

Inside, I felt like I'd stepped into a different world. The walls were lined with shelves from floor to ceiling and full of strange ingredients, tools, and potions. As Max urged me toward the back of the shop, the thick scent of herbs, spices, and oils filled my senses.

Rich, dark wood covered the upper sections of the walls, etched with intricate designs and adorned with shelves full of small bottles and jars. Brightly colored liquids and dried roots dangled from the ceiling. Mortar and pestles sat beside clear bottles full of colorful stones and powder.

I wanted to check everything out, but Max hurried me to the back and a counter. A tall elf stood behind it, watching us with one lifted eyebrow—Tylik, the elf looking for someone to get married right away—who would not be me.

"How may I help you?" he asked quite pleasantly.

"We need a few items," I said, my voice shaking. It wasn't often I went to the store for dragon's blood.

Max stood beside me like a bodyguard, scowling. Surely the elf was intimidated by such a massive green orc.

"I see," Tylik said, blinking slowly. And maybe he wasn't intimidated. "What do you need?" He tugged on his pristine white smock top.

I took in his long gold hair. Like the other day, he'd pulled some up in a man bun at the back of his head, leaving the rest to hang around his shoulders. I had to admit, he had interesting pointy ears. Cute ears as far as ears went. Not marriage material for me, but I was pretty sure he'd charm someone else into walking down the aisle.

"We have a list." I laid it on the counter and pushed it toward him.

"Please fill the list," Max said firmly.

"I would be happy to do so, especially for you, Maxon, since you so kindly helped me construct my home, but she is human. I am not allowed to go against any rules in the newly formed treaty. I do extend my apology, however."

"We're getting these items for her boyfriend," Max said. "I believe you know Raze?"

The elf sucked in his breath. "She's with . . . Raze?"

"I am," I said. "You don't need to worry about me suddenly taking up spellcasting."

"I appreciate your honesty." Tylik lifted the paper and studied it. "Very well. I am happy to help. I don't have dragon blood. They're on strike and refusing to donate."

"Is there a good substitution?" Max asked. "We need it for a spell, as you've probably assumed."

"I assume you're concocting a compulsion spell of some sort?"

"Yes," Max said. "What will work instead?"

"There aren't many substitutions for dragon blood but allow me to take care of the rest of your list, and then I shall look around." Tylik took a jar from a shelf behind him, then others, slowly packing some in vials or containers and placing them in a silver bag.

"We still have a few drops of dragon blood left," Max said.

Tylik nodded slowly. "That may be enough. Contract negotiations are underway with the dragons. Would you like . . .?"

"What?" Max asked.

A sigh slipped from his throat. "Never mind." He finished placing everything in the bag, then turned and studied each item on the shelf. "I'm afraid I don't have anything else that will work. I do apologize again." He folded the top of the bag and handed it to me. "My lady." He gave me a bow. "I wish you all the best."

Lady? "Uh, thanks."

He seemed like a sweet guy, if stilted and formal. I

hoped he found someone to marry him soon, and while he was at it, I hoped he fell in love, because I adored happy endings.

"If you'll excuse me," Tylik said, stepping away from the counter. He pivoted and strode through a doorway into a back room.

"We need to pay him," I said.

"He'll send Raze a bill." Max took my arm. "Let's get this stuff home."

As we left the shop, I peered back.

Tylik had returned. He watched us, his sapphire gaze full of more emotion than I'd seen there before.

The primary thing I noted was concern.

CHAPTER 30
RAZE

We heard the sirens before the lights arced across the back of Paige's vehicle.

"Shit," Paige said, slinking down in her seat. "It's the cops." She guided the car into the breakdown lane and put it in park.

We waited for the cop car to pass, but it pulled in behind us, the lights still flashing across the night.

"Double shit," she hissed. "Act natural. Let me do the talking."

Darrow put his hand on hers clenching the steering wheel. "I can handle it."

"No!" She lowered her voice as a door opened and shut in the vehicle behind us. "You don't like turning people to stone. You've vowed you'd only do it when one of us is in grave danger."

"Which we might be," he said softly. "I'll protect you. I love you, Paige."

"I'll handle this," I said, opening the back door and prying myself out of the tight space.

Sheriff Venom sauntered toward me; his dark eyebrows lifted. His sharp gaze shot from me to Harris's stone body lying across the roof racks.

"Care to explain what's going on here?" he asked, stopping in front of me. He leaned around me to scowl at Paige and Darrow, both of whom were peering through her open window.

"Well," I said. How could I explain? I wasn't confident I could stretch the little bit of grace he'd given me at the restaurant.

"That's the human male that was trying to mess with your female," Venom pointed out, his brow ridge lifting.

"Yes." I nodded, though my word should be enough. I was nervous. Nothing wrong with that. We were breaking every law in and outside the book by turning Harris to stone and kidnapping him. "We're taking Harris for a ride."

"And he just happens to enjoy doing so on the roof." Venom's lips thinned. "In stone form." He scowled toward the driver's window. "Medusa. Thought so."

"*Gorgon*," Darrow said. "I'm a gorgon. There's a difference."

"I'm very well aware of the difference," Venom said. "Do you think I left the underworld yesterday?"

"Didn't you?" Paige asked.

"No." His gaze returned to me, and I was grateful he seemed to like ogres. "Explain."

Maybe I should tell him everything. He'd been

sympathetic the other night. Surely, he'd be okay with how we were handling this now?

"Harris wouldn't stop bothering Elisa," I said, bracing my hip against the back of Paige's car.

"He's a real jerk," Paige chimed in. "Like an asshole."

Venom sucked in a breath between his fangs.

"He threatened her dog," I said.

"What?" Venom barked.

"He broke into her apartment and trashed most of her things. He pinned her dog under a laundry basket, but the threat there was obvious. He hates Chickpea and told Elisa in the past he'd be happy to dispose of her pet if she didn't behave."

Venom scowled at Harris. "I don't condone anyone mistreating females and pets," he snarled. "You get that?"

Could Harris hear what was being said? If I were him, I'd be cowering inside the stone.

"I brought Elisa to my place. I'm going to protect her with my life," I vowed.

"I assume you decided to take matters into your own hands and do this." Venom slashed his claws toward the statue lying across the car's roof. "Rather than notify me?"

I hadn't thought of calling him, actually. "I apologize."

Venom started pacing, growls ripping up his throat.

A car passed us, the driver noting the tall, red-skinned, horned demon snarling at the moon, Harris, and probably me. He jerked his vehicle so far to the left he nearly drove it into a ditch.

Venom glared at the car and the tires squealed, the driver slamming his foot on the gas pedal.

"Yeah, slow down," Venom bellowed, shaking his fist. He pointed his gaze my way. If I was a lesser ogre, I'd cringe. "If I wasn't dealing with you and this," his claw jerked toward Harris again, "I'd hunt them down and explain to them why they need to slow down."

"It's dangerous to drive fast."

"They might hit a deer or even a rabbit."

Rabbit? I shook my head. It didn't matter.

"We're going to perform a spell on Harris," I said.

Venom stops moving. "What kind of spell?"

"A simple one."

"What kind?" He growled. "You know only witches and elite elves are allowed to perform magic. And when I say allowed, I mean humans permit it to happen as long as it's not directed at them. For example, Harris now turned to stone."

"It wasn't a spell."

Darrow got out of the car and came around to join us. When Paige attempted to open her door, he hip-checked it shut and leaned against it.

"Hey," she huffed. "I want to help."

He bent toward her and kissed her cheek. "You help best by staying in the car. Let us handle this."

"Let the men handle it," she said in a sing-song tone. "I'm well able to handle demons."

"That's what they all say," Venom said with a flash of

his glowing eyes. "There was one woman . . . Yeah, I'm not going there. Suffice it to say I have a healthy respect for females."

"And pets," I pointed out.

"Exactly. Don't come after either of them, and you'll get along fine in this town." His half-smile fled, his face taking on an expression harder than Harris's current form. "What spell do you plan to perform?"

"A forget spell so he no longer remembers Elisa," I said.

Darrow's hair whirled around his head like sea grass in a tropical storm.

"You need dragon blood," Venom pointed out.

"I've done the spell before," I said.

"Did it work?" His brow lifted, and he studied my face. "Hold on. Do I know you?"

"We met at the Horny Café the other night."

He tapped his chin. "No, I know you from someplace else."

"I'm an ogre. A simple ogre." I was trying to be simple, that is.

Darrow snorted, suggesting Trevor had shared my family history. I wasn't trying to keep my background hidden. I just felt squirmy when I shared it.

"It's not that, but I'll figure it out," Venom said. "Did your spell work? You haven't answered my question."

"I suppose so," I said, splaying my hands wide. "I'm wearing shorts, not a suit."

"Why would you wear a suit to a kidnapping?"

Good question. "The spell worked." I'd barely thought of my father lately, a welcome reprieve.

"You have enough supplies to perform the spell a second time?" Venom asked. "Stuff like that isn't easy to come by."

"Max and Elisa went to Mystic Mixtures to get more," I said.

"Max is the orc running the construction business."

"Yes. His wife, Chastity, remained with our friends to purify the site where we'll perform the spell. I told them how to do it."

"Ah, I know who you are now," Venom said, his eyes flashing again before the light blazing behind them settled to a low simmer. "I will permit *you* to perform the spell."

"Thank you."

A snarl ripped through him. "Don't stand there." His claws flicked out. "Get back to your place and do it before anyone else sees the look of terror on that statue's face."

CHAPTER 31

ELISA

"Incoming," Raze called out as he strode into his backyard through the gate with stone Harris projecting off either side of his shoulder like a thick gray fencepost. I wasn't going to ask why he'd been turned to stone and wasn't instead trussed up and squealing.

Darrow's grim expression did not invite questions.

Fortunately, the lights at the back of the house lit up the area enough to watch whatever might come next.

"Good timing," Goreg said. "We just finished purifying the fire pit and area around it." He took their tools over to the small back deck and laid them on the ground beside it.

Storm and Luna had returned to their frisbee game, and Chickpea happily zipped back and forth between them, barking.

"You need help there?" Max asked Raze, rising from the lawn chair he'd placed beside Chastity's. She held their daughter, who sat on her lap facing outward, kicking her legs and squealing again. She must've had a power nap, because she was raring to go again.

"No, thanks," Raze said. "Got it." He carefully lowered Harris to his feet near the firepit, stuffing a few bricks beneath one of Harris's feet to keep him from toppling.

Chickpea snarled and raced over to Harris, stopping a few feet away to growl. I stooped down and held my hand out to him, but he tiptoed over to Harris instead, looking particularly jaunty with his new red bow.

After sniffing Harris, Chickpea lifted his leg and peed on my ex's ankle.

"Way to go, Chickpea. Revenge is sweet, buddy, isn't it?" I said with a laugh.

My dog trotted over and flopped in the grass by my feet.

"I've got to say, he looks quite tame now," Luna said, strolling around Harris, avoiding the wet spot near his foot. "Can he hear what we're saying?"

"He can," Raze said. "Otherwise, he wouldn't hear the spell."

Luna shot me a grin. "Want to kick him? Now's the time."

"I'll pass." I'd be happy if I never went near him again.

"I could do it for you," she said grimly.

Her brother was pretty much mafia, and he'd had plans for Luna, so she could be equating Harris with him. I'd only heard parts of her story. Something about him wanting to marry her off to a creepy guy running an opposing faction. Luna wouldn't have fared well, just like the guy's prior wives.

When her brother arrived here with his minions to collect her, everyone showed up to help her and Storm fight them off. Darrow turned the bad guys to stone, and Venom took Luna's brother somewhere. He hadn't been seen since.

A shiver tracked through me. Venom might be a gorgeous demon with muscles upon muscles and majestic horns, but I wouldn't want to cross him. Whoever dated him would have to give it back as fast as he dished it out, or he'd run right over them.

"I'll head into the house to prepare myself," Raze said, his gaze lingering on me. "I have to do this part alone. I'm sorry."

"It's okay," I said. "I'll wait here." I grabbed a beer from the cooler, popped the top, and took a long swallow. "It's almost like a party, right?" My voice came out jittery.

Raze strode around the firepit and took the beer, placing it on a table. He lifted me off my feet, giving me a long, smoldering kiss that made me forget where we were, what was going on, and what my name was. It settled into my bones like fire smoldering beneath the ground, waiting for a gasp of air to burst into flame.

"It'll be okay," he whispered, kissing me again quickly. "I won't be long." He lowered me to my feet and strode over to the table where we'd set up our supplies. "Were you able to get more dragon blood?"

"Tylik was all out," I said. "You mentioned you had a few drops left?"

He frowned. "I do, but I'm not sure it's enough."

"We'll make it work," Max said.

With a nod, Raze went inside.

Storm and Luna started playing frisbee again with Chickpea racing back and forth between them.

Max joined Chastity and took Sydnee into his arms, holding her up over his head while she chortled and kicked her legs in the air.

Darrow tinkered with the list of ingredients, shifting them around on the tray, Paige stood near him.

Violet and Goreg stacked kindling and scrunched paper in the firepit, getting it ready, and I joined them in time to place a final piece of wood on the pile. I remained on the opposite side of the pit from Harris, and I was grateful he was looking toward Goreg and Violet's B&B and not in my direction. If things went well, he'd soon look at me as if he'd never seen me before.

Raze came out of his house wearing only a strip of material wrapped around his waist. From its position, it must be giving him a wedgie in the back. I gaped, because he was as gorgeous as always.

Paige whistled.

Luna grinned.

And Chastity nudged Max's side. "Dress like that later, would you?"

He leaned over and gave her a long kiss.

Color rose into Raze's face as we continued to stare.

"The spell works best if I'm naked, but this should be okay."

Yeah, mixed company meant no stripping down to nothing.

"Do you want us to leave?" Darrow asked. "I could return once the spell's done to unlock him."

"I want to watch," Paige said, Luna nodding along with her.

"It'll work whether you're here or not, so you can remain," Raze said solemnly. He lowered a container onto the tray with the other items. "Moonflower petals. I keep them in the fridge." He got to work, lighting the fire. It crackled gleefully, as if it knew what he'd soon ask of it. "Could someone turn off the outside lights?"

Chastity hurried over and shut them off, leaving us with moonlight and the fire to see by.

With the tray in his hands, Raze sat beside the firepit. We crowded around, remaining beyond the purified area as he drew a pattern in the dirt and placed a teal-colored candle in the middle of the symbol. Once it was lit, he put moonflower petals around the candle. A soft hum filled the air.

Luna grinned at Storm, who drew her close for a quick kiss.

I lifted and kissed Chickpea, who licked my chin.

Raze tossed powder into the flames, and green and pink lights shot into the night sky.

He removed the stopper from the top of the vial containing dragon blood, carefully easing a drop onto the flame. Rising to his feet, he bowed toward the candle, holding the position.

The flame roared, arching up, taking on the form of a dragon made of flickering gold and orange lights.

"Wow," Luna whispered.

Everyone else remained silent, staring at the flaming apparition that undulated, whipping back and forth in front of Raze.

"What do you will?" the firedragon asked in a low, growly voice.

"Greetings," Raze said. "My will unfolds. What we seek behold. Banish this male's thoughts from far and low," he tapped Harris's arm. "Never to think of my love, Elisa, again."

"As you—" A pop, and the dragon disappeared, fizzling down into the candle.

CHAPTER 32

RAZE

"That's it?" Elisa asked softly, creeping around the fire. She remained well away from Harris. "It's done? He won't remember me any longer?"

Joy filled her voice, and I hated that I was about to steal that away.

"The dragon disappeared before finishing," Max said. "It didn't work, did it, Raze?"

"Not enough blood," I snarled, upending the vial. Nothing more came out. "We need more dragon blood."

"I believe I can be of assistance," someone said.

We turned to find Sheriff Venom strolling into the yard. He stopped beside the fire and huffed, shaking his head.

"We're out of dragon blood, and Tylik told us the dragons are on strike," Max said.

"I have something better," Venom said, his smile as sly as his namesake.

"You've got an in with a dragon?" I asked. Frustration

poured through me, and my eyes must be glowing bright red.

"Nah," Venom said, holding up his hand. "Demon blood."

I frowned. "I've never performed a spell with demon blood."

Venom snorted. "Because no demon would ever offer it."

"Why are you offering your blood for this spell?" I asked.

"To help her." His gaze fell on Elisa. "And every woman like her who's been harmed by a jerk like him." His foot snapped out, cracking against Harris's leg. Harris toppled over, landing hard on the ground.

Chickpea strutted over to Harris, woofed in his face, then scampered over to sit beside Venom, staring up at him with complete adoration.

"Hurry up and prick my finger before I change my mind," Venom snarled. "I've got plans tonight."

"A date?" Chastity asked, her head tilting.

"I don't date. Not since *her*."

Curiosity poured through me, but I would not ask who he was speaking of. Was she still as haunted by him as he was about her?

I grabbed the knife off the table. "Do you want to poke your finger, or shall I do it?"

"Get everything ready again. I'll do it." He took the blade from me with a twist of his lips and laid the sharp edge near the inside of his forearm.

"Ready," I said a moment later. I bowed toward the flickering candle.

A quick slice, and red blood trickled across Venom's arm. Tendrils of smoke coiled off it, releasing the smell of brimstone.

I'd never seen anything like this before, and I knew to my dying day, I never would again.

He leaned over and blood dripped onto the candle.

A shape erupted from the flame, and Venom reeled backward, putting ten feet or so between him and the . . .

"A demon?" I bellowed, staring at the apparition forming above the candle.

"If you use dragon blood, you summon a dragon," Venom said softly. "Demon blood summons *a demon.*"

"What do ya want?" the demon snarled, glaring at each and every one of us. Only Sydnee didn't cringe. In fact, she shot him a big grin and cooed.

I spoke the words of the spell, requesting Harris forget about Elisa.

"As you wish, so it shall be." The demon released a cackle.

Sydnee kicked her feet and squealed along with him.

I looked from the demon to Elisa, then to Harris.

"Have you moved past her yet, Venom?" the flame demon asked.

"No," Venom snapped, still staying well away from the fire.

"Moved past who?" I asked. Everyone else stared at the flame demon, rapt.

"No one," he said softly. The strangest look filled

Venom's eyes. Our surly, snarly demon *liked* whoever she was.

Maybe even loved her.

The flame demon's gaze fell on me. "Your spell has worked. Release the stone man and let him return from whence he came." A blink, and the demon fizzled, sucked back into the candle.

The flame winked out, leaving only the cackle of the fire, and my friends and I crowded around it.

"Well, I'm amazed," Luna said. "That was something else."

"I can release him?" Darrow asked me, and I nodded.

A blink, and Harris's stony exterior started to crack. The fissures widened and spread faster until skin burst from beneath the stone, fusing together to reform the ass I'd still love to punch.

Harris blinked at the sky. He sat up and peered around my backyard. "Who are all of you, and where am I?"

His gaze skimmed over Elisa as if he'd never seen her before in his life.

"You . . . stopped by to deliver some fliers," I said, helping Harris stand.

"Why are you almost naked?" he asked, tugging on the hem of his shirt. "Aren't the mosquitoes biting your ass?"

His words broke the tension thriving in the air, and we all laughed. Soon, we were crying from laughter while Harris blinked at us.

"I assume I should leave then," he said.

"You should." I took his arm and hustled him toward the gate. "Allow me to show you the way out. I'll call a ride to pick you up and take you to your car."

After leaving him sitting out front and calling a Lyft, I returned to the backyard, wiping my hands together. I strode over to Elisa and held out my arms.

She jumped into them, her arms wrapping around my shoulders.

"Harris will leave me alone forever," she said with so much happiness that it made my chest ache. "It's finally over."

I scrunched forward to kiss her. "Actually, love, everything is just beginning. You. Me. Us."

CHAPTER 33

EPILOGUE
ELISA

A few days later.

Because he looked amazing in his Ogre Games costume, I wanted to lick Raze. But I suspected our friends and everyone sitting in the bleachers around us might not only chuckle if they saw me doing it, but they'd remind me this was not the right time.

"Welcome to the Ogre Games!" the announcer shouted in the field below us.

We sat on wooden bleachers overlooking a field full of mud with a two-story platform on one side holding judges and the ogre MC.

The crowd went wild, and we leapt to our feet, lifting our hands. Once we'd finished a few waves, we sat, waiting to hear what came next.

"There you all are," Raze's mom, Annalisa, said, standing at the end of the aisle.

"Aunt Annalisa," Raze's cousin, Trevor, cried, springing to his feet. He and his wife, Monica, sat on our left, closest to the aisle. Trevor lifted her and spun her around, somehow not losing his feet or disturbing anyone around them.

I tried not to gape at how he was dressed. After all, Raze wore the same thing, as did most of the crowd, a mix of male and female monsters, from gargoyles to ogres to a centaur or two—though the last appeared to be confused about which end to wear their leather, kilt-like skirt. A few centaurs wore it over their hindquarters, which didn't cover much since the kilt dangled. Others opted to wear pants on their back end and the kilt below their chest, covering the top of their front legs.

Women wore leather bras in addition to kilts, and I had major envy, because I was still dressed in jeans and a t-shirt. Raze had promised we'd buy me an outfit from one of the vendors hawking wares in the open field behind the stands, but we hadn't had the chance to go shopping yet.

I was going to participate. Women and men competed against each other, so that should be interesting to see.

"While our team is setting up the field," the MC said as Trevor returned to his seat, "I'll explain the upcoming event." He continued speaking, telling everyone how the game would be scored and played.

Annalisa scooted past him to sink down in the open spot on the other side of Raze. She leaned past him and grinned my way, showing off her glorious tusks. Her long, straight black hair made her resemble most ogres, and she also had horns and coppery-gold skin. With a shake of her head, she rose and moved past Raze, squishing her butt down between us while he smiled and shifted over to make room.

"As you know, I'm Annalisa, Raze's mom," she said. Her elbow gouged Raze's side. "This lug here should've formally introduced me much sooner."

"Sorry, Mom," Raze said, shooting me a sheepish grin. "I figured you two already knew each other."

"I'm not making her a sandwich," Annalisa said with a roll of her eyes just like Raze's.

I gaped, trying to figure out what to say that would show well and not make me come across . . . well, stupid, I guessed. I wanted to appear worthy of her precious son.

"He mentioned he was seeing you," she said. "And while I was stunned that he didn't bring you by my place immediately, I'm going to forgive him. This time." She poked his side again, but he just grinned indulgently and it made me know she was special. "Don't do this again. Although," she smiled my way again, "I suspect there won't be a next time to formally meet his girlfriend."

"We're getting married, Mom," Raze said.

"What?" She started to rise before sinking back onto the bench. "Way to share something important, son." Her gaze swung back to me. "We need to chat and soon, but for now, it's almost time to compete!" She also wore a kilt in bright pink stripes, plus a matching bra. Her attention dropped down my front. "Are you competing too?"

"I want to. We were going to get me an outfit before the second event."

"Well, let me take you." Before I could say a word, she rose and swept me up with her, dragging me down the aisle to the stairs. I waved at Raze, who grinned.

In no time, we reached the ground, and she tugged me around the stands to the open meadow full of vendors.

Shooting her a grin, I picked up my pace to half-jog beside her. Man, she was tall and sturdy. And gorgeous. If I didn't know she was his mom, I might suspect she was his older sister.

"Hold every horse in the place." She paused, staring across the meadow, her hand lifting to point. "Who's *that*?"

There were many "thats" here.

"Are you talking about anyone in particular?" I asked, wondering why one person had drawn her attention.

"The gargoyle," she breathed.

At least there was only one gargoyle in the meadow, making it easy to identify him.

"That's Murtik," I said. "One of Goreg's brothers."

"Violet's Goreg?"

"That's the one." Was there any other gargoyle named Goreg?

"I need to meet him." Determination filled her voice. "But let's get your outfit first. After you've changed, I'll return you to Raze and hunt down Murtik." She shot me a grin. "He's kinda cute, don't you think?" Her face fell. "Wait. He's not dating anyone, is he?"

"He has a reputation for dating lots of women, but as far as I know, he's not with anyone at the moment." Was that a polite enough way to tell her Murtik could be compared to a cat on the prowl? I wouldn't want Annalisa to think he was prime dating material. Although, most guys just needed to meet the right person for that to happen. For him, that person could be Annalisa.

"I'll introduce you, if you'd like," I said.

She linked her arm through mine. "I'd love that. This way, my dear."

She guided me to a shop selling competitor outfits in varying sizes, and I found one I liked. I wasn't sure about letting my belly hang out, but no one else seemed to care. Monsters came in all sizes and shapes, and I'd yet to meet anyone who gave a damn what others looked like.

I dressed in the changing area and the yeti vendor put my clothing inside a bag, handing it to me with a wink and a smile. "Have fun!"

"Is it time?" Annalisa asked, staring toward Murtik, who flirted with the ten females of various species crowding around him.

"Are you sure you want to meet him when he's . . ."

"Trying to lure a couple females into his bed?" She

shot me a full-tusked grin. "Sure. Watch me in action." Taking my hand, she strutted toward him.

When he saw her approaching, he frowned. As if willed by some invisible force, he shifted the other females aside and stepped out from among them. Alone, he stopped, watching as we approached, his eyes never leaving Annalisa.

Whoa. I'd never seen Murtik act this way.

We stopped in front of him, and I felt a tad like a shadow standing beside Annalisa, though I didn't need his attention or appreciation. I had Raze, and he was the only person I'd want for the rest of my life.

"Hi, Murtik," I said. I *had* promised to introduce her. "This is Raze's . . ." Maybe it would be best not to name relationships. I'd leave that to her. "This is Annalisa." I thought of adding that she was an ogre, but that was apparent. "Annalisa? This is Murtik." I didn't know his other names.

"Murtik Eskaban Odran," he said, taking her extended hand. His wings shot out, nearly impaling a passing elf couple as he bent over her fingers to kiss them. "A delight to meet you, Royal Mother."

Royal Mother? Was the title part of ogre culture?

"You know who I am?" Annalisa fluttered her lashes and color seeped into her cheeks. She couldn't stop staring at Murtik. Fortunately, he seemed to feel the same.

"How could I not know the former queen of the ogres?" he said.

I frowned at her. "Former queen?"

"Didn't Raze mention it?" Annalisa said. "He abdicated, but my son would otherwise be king."

King.

I felt like I'd stumbled into a tunnel and couldn't figure my way out. That explained his formality and wearing suits all the time.

Who woulda thought?

"I'm going to get back to Raze," I told Annalisa.

She dragged her gaze from Murtik. "I'll come with you." Her head tilted his way. "I'm sure I'll see you again, Murtik Eskaban Odran."

"I assure you, you will." He watched her raptly, completely ignoring the females fluttering around behind him. Had I seen him meet his match? Time would tell.

We walked across the meadow, nearly running into Chastity while weaving through the crowd.

"Hey," Chastity said. She stood in line with Max's parents, Ulgritte and BB. Ahead, a troll roasted various meats and vegetables on sticks over a fire behind a counter.

BB held Sydnee. "Aren't you a sweetie?" he asked, as if she could answer.

She cooed and kicked her feet.

He kissed her cheek and gazed adoringly at Chastity. I'd heard he was mean to her when they first met, but whatever their issues, they'd smoothed things out. Every time I'd seen him in town, he was buying her flowers or something pretty. And he told everyone how wonderful she was.

After chatting with them for a few minutes, we left them to eat their meal and returned to the stands, finding Raze and our friends gathering near the entrance to the game field.

"Just in time," Raze said, gazing at me with appreciation. He'd taken off his glasses and wore contacts, and while he looked amazing without them, I loved him just as much with glasses. "The second event is about to get started."

I peered past him, frowning. "There's a lot of mud in there." When had they flooded the field with more gook?

"Mud's a lot of fun," he said with a wiggle of his brow. "Maybe we can roll around in it later."

"But we'll get dirty." Why was I protesting? It sounded like a great time.

He leaned close to my ear, lowering his voice. "You know I love to get dirty."

With him, I adored getting dirty too.

"We can use the hot springs pools to get clean after," he added.

"Where you can explain why your mom mentioned you were the king of the ogres?"

"Ah, my not-so-secret is out?" He watched my face. Did he think I'd be angry?

Wait. He'd abdicated, so he was no longer king, but was I now sort of a former queen? Ha. I could deal with that.

"I heard you talking about getting dirty." Raze's mom

shook her finger at him, but her bright laughter rang out. "None of that smutty talk around your mom, son."

He chuckled. "It's not anything you wouldn't do." Raze shot me a wink. I loved how close he was with his mom, how welcoming she was to me, and well, I just loved her already.

"I'm up for hot springs after the mud event," I said.

"It's a date," he said, squeezing my hand.

"How do we play this game?" I asked, watching as they set up rings on posts here and there across the field. Someone else brought out a big bag of colorful balls and placed it near the wall. "I missed the announcement."

"We have to run through the mud and put as many balls through hoops as possible." He heeled off his shoes. "Barefoot."

Oh, jeez. But when in Monsterville . . . I kicked off my sneakers and sashayed around Raze while he watched, his eyes gleaming with a light that wouldn't be extinguished until we'd been alone for a considerable amount of time.

"We're going to sit and cheer you on," Darrow said with a grin. He and Paige returned to the stands, holding hands.

"Are we competing with each other or as a team?" I asked.

"Unless you'd like to compete with me," Vrok said, coming over to stand beside Raze. His dragonette rode on his naked shoulder, and when it saw us looking, it fluttered its wings.

I looked around but didn't see Margie.

"It's truly over," he said softly, all humor fleeing his green face. Sadness filled his eyes. "I suppose it's for the best, but . . ."

It hurt. I gave him a hug, something everyone needed every now and then. His dragonette stared down at me before giving me a little nod.

Releasing him, I stepped back.

"Nice to see you, Vrok," Raze said, bracing his palm on the other guy's shoulder.

"All the best with the game," Vrok said. "I need to see if anyone needs a partner." With a nod our way, he wove through the crowd.

My heart squeezed tight. Being in love with Raze made me want everyone else to feel the same. I hoped Vrok healed and could find someone new.

"As for teams, love," Raze grabbed my hand as the gate swept open behind him, "It's a free-for-all, but you and I will compete together."

Everyone raced into the arena and rushed toward the balls.

Our friends shouted and laughed around us, slipping in the thick mud, falling to splatter it everywhere.

Gunner held Rylee's hand, tugging her along, just like Trevor and Monica.

Goreg had the advantage of his wings. Wearing a white kilt that would soon be mud-brown, he flew above the muck, carrying Violet and their ball.

Murtik remained behind Annalisa, his gaze locked on her pretty form. Their developing relationship was going to be fun to watch.

And Storm had shifted into wolf form. He ran with Luna beside him, her hair streaming out like a flag.

When we reached the balls, Raze swept me up in his arms and leapt toward the big cluster, landing with a huge splat in the mud nearby. His feet went out from beneath him, and he skidded to the ground, rolling until he came to a stop. He braced himself over me.

Grinning, he swiped at my cheek. "You're getting dirty, love. I can't wait to rub a cloth all over you to get you clean."

My pulse thrummed, and my heart skipped around, banging against my ribs. "Maybe *I'm* going to wipe each speck of mud off *you* first."

"We'll do it together." He kissed me quickly, then sprang up and off me, frowning down at where I lay in the mud. "Don't just lounge there, sweet. Time to grab balls and compete."

As I struggled to rise, he swept me up and spun me around, not caring about balls, mud, or even the competition. He kept kissing me, and frankly, he could do that all day long. Who needed a game when I had him?

But I couldn't stop laughing, and it broke through our kiss.

"I don't believe you're taking me seriously," he said with a grin.

"Do you want me to?"

"Actually, I don't. I'm enjoying relaxing and having fun with you."

I felt the same.

There was nothing better than spending time with my ogre king.

I hope you enjoyed Raze & Elisa's story!

Have you checked out the rest of the Monsterville world?
Candy For My Orc Boss, Max & Chastity
Orc Me Baby One More Time, Gunner & Rylee
Gargoyles Just Want to Have Fun, Goreg & Violet
Don't Go Knotting My Heart, Storm & Luna
Whose Bed Have Your Claws Been Under, Darrow &
Paige
Uptown Ogre, Raze & Elisa
My Orc-y Breaky Heart, Vrok & Seyla
Hold Me Closer, Fiery Phoenix, Nyxor & Brooke
& Who Let the Demon Out?
(Venom & Ali's story)

Turn the page for Chapter 1 of
Oops, I Elf'd it Again.
Tylik's looking for someone to marry him right away.
Will he find true love instead?

My Orc-y Breaky Heart follows in

my Monsterville, USA world,
when Vrok meets the love of his life in Seyla.

Would you like a FREE book?
Just sign up for my newsletter, and
I'll send you Escorting the Alien,
a complete, HEA romance.

About the Author

Ava Ross is a two-time *USA Today* Bestselling author who has written numerous titles, all of them featuring sweet and steamy romance. She fell for men with unusual features when she first watched Star Wars, where alien creatures have gone mainstream. She lives in New England with her husband (who is sadly not an alien, though he is still cute in his own way), her kids, and a few assorted pets.

SERIES BY AVA

Mail-Order Brides of Crakair

Brides of Driegon

Fated Mates of the Ferlaern Warriors

Fated Mates of the Xilan Warriors

Holiday with a Cu'zod Warrior

Galaxy Games

*Alien Warrior Abandoned/
Shattered Galaxies*

Beastly Alien Boss

Bride of the Fae

A Sci-Fi Holiday Tail

Monsterville, USA

Monster on Board
(co-written with Alana Khan)

A Monster Worth Fighting For
(Monster Between the Sheets)

Love at First Orc

Third Galaxy on the Left

Monster Mate Hunt

You can find my books on Amazon.

OOPS, I ELF'D IT AGAIN

I'm teaching a gorgeous elf how to fit in with humans and now I'm falling in love.

With thirty-six looming on my horizon, I'm determined to have a child. I don't need romance. I don't need love. And I definitely don't need a happily ever after.

When my friend talks me into attending an elf ball at an estate in Monsterville, promising I'll find a guy there who'll give me what I'm seeking, I agree to go with her.

I'm barely there when I fall into the arms of the most gorgeous elf I've ever seen, Tylik. He's the LOTR elf of my dreams, so it's a good thing I've sworn off romance.

Tylik needs someone to teach him how to fit in with human society. I need a bundle of joy. We'll help each other, then end things with no looking back.

But between teaching Tylik how to drive and showing him that ice cream is amazing, I fall in love. What if he doesn't feel the same?

Oops, I Elf'd it Again, Book 7 in the Monsterville, USA Series, is a spicy monster romcom. Each book is stand-alone and best if read in order (see below). Expect romantic hijinks with monsters, heat, and a happily ever after.

Turn the page for Chapter 1 . . .
Check out the entire Monsterville world!
Candy for my Orc Boss
Orc Me Baby One More Time
Gargoyles Just Want to Have Fun
Don't Go Knotting My Heart
Whose Bed Have Your Claws Been Under?
Uptown Ogre
Oops, I Elf'd it Again
My Orc-y Breaky Heart
Hold Me Closer, Fiery Phoenix
Who Let the Demon Out?

CHAPTER 1
KATE

I was not a princess, but I was going to a ball. An elf ball! My bestie, Seyla, hoped to find someone to love. As for me, I was looking for a baby daddy.

We rode in the back of a Lyft, the driver taking the main road into the mountains surrounding Monsterville, aiming for the elf duchess's estate. Our puffy gowns billowed around us, and my feet ache from the tiny slippers Seyla had insisted I wear to this illustrious event.

They'd built the estate in the hills with the help of an orc guy who owned a construction company in town, adding a dash of magic. How else could it have been erected so quickly?

Anticipation rocketed through my belly, and Seyla must've felt the same because she kept wrangling my hand and grinning.

Our troll driver peered at us in his rearview mirror. Pressing down on the gas pedal, he urged the vehicle up a winding road, slowly taking us through the dense forest where I'd heard wolf shifter packs and a yeti still lived.

We'd cracked a window, and warm, summery air billowed across us, cooling my overheated body. The fresh scent of pine trees filled my senses, and when we reached the peak of one of the lower hills, we spied our destination; the gilded, four-story building perched on the top of one of the crests.

"Tell me again why we're doing this?" I said for what had to be the thousandth time.

When Seyla smiled, the dimple in her right cheek showed. "Because we're Cinderella without the stepsisters. Commoners attending an elf ball."

"We're human, not necessarily commoners."

She sniffed. "To the elves, we're probably very common."

"The elves are probably right." Regarding me anyway. My upbringing had been simple and poor, though that wasn't uncommon in this country.

As for Seyla, she was wealthy, though you wouldn't know it. My friend was anything but snooty.

"Tonight, you're a princess," she said. "I'll be your lady's maid."

"Ha ha. More like the other way around."

She rolled her pretty brown eyes framed with incredibly long lashes and smoothed her long brown hair shot through with naturally golden highlights. If she wasn't such a nice person, I'd hate her for her lashes alone. To make mine look good, I had to wear fifty coats of mascara or attach fake ones. And forget brown hair gleaming in the sunlight. I was stuck with the same auburn as my mom.

"I'm worried I'm going to trip and fall in this gown," I said. "You know I don't do fancy." I was more a jeans and t-shirt kind of girl.

"I'll hold on to you."

Until she was surrounded by guys, the norm with my friend. She would barely see them, and she'd be embarrassed to draw their attention. Meanwhile, I'd awkwardly lurk in the shadows of her light despite her trying to drag me into the sunshine to stand beside her. "It's nice to look pretty every now and then, isn't it?"

"It is."

She leaned against my shoulder. "Thank you for coming with me."

Our vehicle swooped down the hill and up the next, and in no time, we glided along a long, paved drive leading to the enormous, ancient-appearing structure. I pressed my face against the window, taking in the huge blocks of white stone making up the soaring stone walls with spires on each corner. A lush green meadow surrounded the castle with a dense forest behind. Rays from the setting sun slanted across the sky, highlighting colorful flowerbeds scattered throughout the landscape.

"We're going to a ball, and I'm going to find the monster of my dreams," she said. "No ifs, ands, or buts."

Ah, monsters . . .

A few years ago, they'd crawled out of the woods and announced they'd been living parallel lives to ours. At first, everyone freaked. I mean, who wouldn't when an orc stomped through town? This explained the yeti sightings through the years, let alone the Loch Ness Monster. They were *all* real. A treaty was formed, and they moved in among us, the majority of them settling in this area.

When Seyla had suggested we move to Monsterville, I'd snickered. But when she'd talked about meeting a nice monster to love forever, I'd caved. I didn't want a long-term relationship, but I'd never hold her back.

It didn't really matter where I lived as long as I was near my best friend.

"You know I'm not looking for a boyfriend or husband," I said. When you loved someone, they left you, like my dad. "I've got one goal." At thirty-five, my clock was ticking. "My eggs are aging and it's time to put one of them to good use."

"Lots of women have kids when they're older, even in their fifties. And if you can't carry one yourself, you can hire a surrogate or try adoption. There are tons of foster kids looking for someone to love."

"I'm not opposed to any of that, but I've set a goal. I can accomplish anything I want to as long as I put my mind to it."

"Your determination is amazing."

"Thank you."

"We'll find a baby daddy for you at the ball." She squinted out the window as the vehicle approached the castle. "If there are no likely prospects, we'll cut out early and watch some movies."

"Mermaid first, I assume."

"Then we'll watch Brave."

My favorite.

"I see myself as Princess Merida—minus the cute shape and princess-ness," I said.

"You're regal."

"Thanks." I stroked my long tresses she'd artfully arranged for me. She said pulling them up made my neck appear swanlike. "I've got her hair."

"Totally."

"It's my one good feature."

"You have tons of good features." She pursed her lips. "You're pretty, brave like the princess, and you're the nicest person I know." She poked my chest gently.

"We just moved to Monsterville so know many people here." We'd packed our things and driven halfway across the country, renting rooms at a cute little B&B run by a human/gargoyle couple, Violet and Goreg. I missed my mom, but it was time I stretched my wings.

Seyla had put a deposit on a house and would move out soon. I'd remain at the B&B until I'd saved enough for an apartment. The B&B wasn't a bad place to live. Eye candy helped; Goreg was a god with wings.

"You know what I mean," she said. "You're amazing. Some monster is going to scoop you up."

"I think the phrase is sweep me off my feet."

"That too."

I shot her a grin. "Thanks, but nope."

"You need to saddle that bad boy and get riding."

"Men are not stallions."

"Around here, they might be. Have you checked out the centaur living down the street?"

I frowned. "I've always wondered about centaurs."

"Ask one on a date. It could be a wild ride."

We both snickered. Talking about a guy's junk was much easier than dealing with it.

"You look wonderful, and every elf in the place is going to notice," she said. "Our gowns are perfect. *We're* perfect."

Thank you, Rylee, for giving me a full-time position —with benefits! —in her cupcake shop/bakery. Otherwise, I wouldn't have been able to afford this gown, even with Seyla's "loan" that wasn't really a loan. As a romance author, she made boatloads of money. She'd paid for half my dress.

I'd have more money in general but my mom needed help. There was nothing wrong with being there for your family.

"I think this is as close as I'm allowed to go," the troll driver said, bringing the vehicle to a stop behind other vehicles discharging guests. "Is this enough?"

"Yes, thanks," I said.

"The elf ball, then, my ladies," he said, sweeping his clawed hand toward the huge stone estate.

"Thank you," Seyla called out in a sing-song voice. "Here we come, elves!"

I liked elves. Lord of the Rings was one of my favorite movies.

The driver backed up and turned, soon zooming down the drive while Seyla and I tiptoed toward the entrance on our heels. We took the broad granite steps to the top and followed other guests toward the big front doors held open by elves with long black hair and pristine tunics with enough gild to fit in a medieval movie.

Seyla paused on the broad stone deck to primp our hair and dresses.

Two elf women to our right glared.

"You're in the way," one said, staring down her hawk-like nose at us.

I gaped at her long, glorious white hair, her teal eyes that almost glowed, and how amazing she looked in her silver gown.

"Come, Drueline," the other woman said in a snooty tone, tugging on her friend's arm. "Ignore the humans."

They sauntered through the front door like runway models.

"Yeah, we'll ignore *them*," Seyla said, fluffing the artfully created curls draping around my shoulders. "Funny how you run into mean girls in every culture. You'd think women would stand up for each other, but no." She smoothed my gown and grinned. "It doesn't matter. You're pure perfection."

"Thanks. So are you."

"You'll find someone tonight. Curl your finger a likely guy's way, take him to the garden for some hot and heavy, then say goodbye."

"I can't do something like that. That would be using someone as a sperm donor without his consent."

"Be honest, then. Tell him you want a baby, but you

don't want commitment, that you won't ask him for child support or any rights."

I frowned. "Will a guy go along with something like that?'

She shrugged. "All you can do is ask."

Short of putting up a notice on the telephone poles in town, *Woman Seeking Sperm Donor, only those uninterested in commitment need apply*, I didn't appear to have many options.

I doubted Monster Mingle, the matchmaking business in town, would fix me up with a monster looking to give me a baby without the marriage, house, and backyard stuff that made my heart eager to run.

"Consider it a bachelorette season only instead of looking for a husband, you're looking for baby-making material."

"No love."

She made an X on her chest. "Emotions are off limits. Make that clear from the start."

As we passed the elves holding the doors open, they bowed. We tap-tap-taped on our heels into an enormous, multi-story foyer. Gold outlined the walls and the arched ceiling three or four stories above us. Magic hung in the air; I could almost feel it shimmering around me.

"That can't be real gold," I whispered to Seyla, nudging my finger toward a satyr statue gleaming in the low lights.

She shrugged and smoothed her gown. She'd dressed in a floor-length, baby blue dress that made her look like a princess.

I wore a dark green dress that was essentially a cliché for a redhead, one with a too-low bodice that barely covered my boobs. As long as I didn't sneeze, they wouldn't pop out.

"Where should we go?" I asked, peering around.

"Up the stairs, ladies," one of the tall elves near the door said, pointing. "Follow the sounds of the crowd." His appreciative gaze glided down Seyla's body, though she didn't appear to notice.

At the top of the stairs, we walked sedately down an ornate hall with marble tiled floors and paintings of stoic elves mounted on the walls. At the end, we came to a large double doorway with huge planters on either side containing potted palms reaching toward the high ceiling. Lilting music, bright chatter, and the clink of glasses drew us toward the room beyond like butterflies to pretty flowers.

We paused in the opening, eyeing the ball in progress.

"Whoa. Monsters," Seyla breathed, taking in golden-furred yetis, short trolls with knobby heads, ogres, orcs, and so many other kinds of monsters I quickly lost count.

And so many elves. Universally tall, they had long hair of every color imaginable, and the males wore tunics that would fit into a fantasy movie. The women wore gowns like ours. They were regal, they stole my breath.

One elf guy caught my eye. He towered over the rest, his broad shoulders filling out his deep blue tunic that matched his sapphire eyes. Some of his silver hair had been pulled up in a man bun at the back of his head, leaving the rest draping around his shoulders.Thranduil anyone?

As if he sensed my attention, his gaze scanned the room and locked on mine. He continued to stare. Heat filled my cheeks. Women of various species fluttered around him, and I could see why. I kinda wanted to hover around him myself.

He disengaged himself from the women and left the ballroom through a door on side before I could head in his direction.

"It's gorgeous here," Seyla sighed.

A table holding drinks and snacks had been set up along the left wall, and I'd head in that direction as soon as one of the numerous monsters staring Seyla's way snagged her attention. A majestic fountain containing a beverage took up the center of the table, guests dipping out glasses before rejoining the crowd.

The far wall was made up of multi-story glass, it overlooked the gardens spreading across an enormous back lawn all the way to the forest. Setting sunlight sparkled on fountains and highlighted numerous statues.

Seyla shot me a nervous smile. "Let's get a drink. I need the boost."

I followed her toward the fountain, but before we got there, a tall, gorgeous elf wearing a dark purple tunic and black pants, with black hair shot through with gold, strutted over to walk beside her.

When she stopped, he bowed and held out his hand. "Would you care to dance?"

She fluttered her hands at her throat and looked at me.

I knew what she was thinking. She didn't want to abandon me.

"Go," I said with an easy smile. "I'll get that drink and hang out."

"You're sure?" she said.

"Totally."

After shooting me a sly grin, she took the elf's hand, and he led her toward the big dance floor in front of the windows.

I skipped the buffet table and drink fountain, scooting along the outside of the room until I reached the door the gorgeous elf had disappeared through.

Because I was curious about where he'd gone, I ducked through the opening, finding myself in a long, gilded hall. I walked along the smooth, marble surface all the way to the end and through a big archway, finding yet another hall stretching to my left and right. After taking a few rights, and then a couple of lefts, I was lost, and no one was ever going to find me.

So much for scouting out potential baby making material.

I was passing yet another open doorway when I spied a giant library through the opening. Totally cool.

Stepping inside, I gasped. I was Belle, and I'd walked into book heaven. Shelves full of colorful books took up three of the four walls of the enormous, multi-story room. On the outer wall, tall windows surrounded with thick ruby drapes looked out at the gardens, and a huge stone fireplace dominated the center of the wall.

I strolled across the right side of the room, tracing my fingers across the spines. So many choices. How could someone decide which to read first?

Voices echoed in the hallway.

Afraid of being caught where I didn't belong, I scurried across the room and ducked behind one of the long, thick drapes.

Someone entered the room, and from the sound, they sat in a chair near the fireplace. Another person joined the first, and his deep, achingly beautiful voice echoed in the room.

I wanted to reveal myself and meet him. He must be one of the painfully gorgeous elves I'd seen in the ballroom.

I waited, remaining still.

Listening.

Get Oops, I Elf'd it Again NOW!